MYSTICAL PHANTASIA

MYSTICAL PHANTASIA

The Tower of Terra

MICHAEL R WELCH

authorHOUSE®

AuthorHouse™ LLC
1663 Liberty Drive
Bloomington, IN 47403
www.authorhouse.com
Phone: 1-800-839-8640

Published by AuthorHouse   10/05/2013

ISBN: 978-1-4772-7003-5 (sc)
ISBN: 978-1-4918-2592-1 (hc)
ISBN: 978-1-4772-7002-8 (e)

Library of Congress Control Number: 2012917067

THE ADVENTURER'S OATH

SET SAIL FOR THE SEA AND THE STARS BEYOND.

PIERCE THE VEIL OF NIGHT TO BREAK FORTH INTO THE MAJESTIC HEAVENS.

SOAR TO THE LIGHT THEREOF
     THAT LIES BEYOND.

WALK THE PATH OF THE ONE STREAMING THROUGH THE GALAXY. ASCEND THE UNIVERSAL ROAD THAT NO OTHER CAN TRANSCEND OR FATHOM.

ASCEND WHAT CANNOT BE TRANSCENDED. TRANSCEND WHAT CANNOT BE ASCENDED. FOREVER FOLLOW THE BANNER THAT WAVES
     TRUE.

Signed,

Platinum M,

The King of Thieves

Prologue

The continent of Deserna had become a war-torn battlefield ravaged by the fear generated from rumors of secret dealings hence a malicious shadow government emerged. It soon toppled the king, taking over and bringing to light the king's faults; however, none of them mentioned his merits in bringing the kingdom back from the brink of a devastating famine and drought that had choked the vast and once-proud land. Working with the people, the king had turned it into a virtual paradise, with lush green fields and a plentiful harvest.

They claimed that the king had been a weak ruler, and that was the reason for Deserna's decline to the state that it was in at the time. However, the king's royal court officials were at odds with one another. Some reached for more wealth and power, while others fought to stop those officials; as a result, internal feuds arose. Some said this was the reason that the continent fell. Others said the continent fell because of the king reducing the size of his military to that of a small kingdom and not a continental empire as the forefathers had left it. Unlike his forefathers, this new king had a strong desire to bring peace to the continent after many years of war and bloodshed. In doing so, however, did he really help the continent to fall? The story of the future of Deserna is now. Slowly, the continent is slipping deeper into darkness because of these actions. But there are whispers in myth and legend of a power that will bestow the user with the might to save Deserna or destroy it—and the universe. This brings us to the mysterious group called the Mappers.

The Mappers are adventurers who secretly move through the background to map planets and worlds beyond anything anyone has ever seen.

Some say to fully destroy the king's power, his family was eliminated by assassins. However, can this be the truth, or is it just mere fabrication and more propaganda spread by the shadow government as a tactic to control all of Deserna? But fear not; the future is always unclear, and many streaming paths open in the most unlikely of events.

All that is known is that the Mappers' chronicles are vast and numerous. These are their stories, which are tied to the fate of the almost lost continent of Deserna.

Contents

—THE HORROR—

I've been on the road for days now, barely sleeping or eating. It's . . . It's been chasing me for days, months . . . Why is it after me—or us? How much longer can I hold out? When we got here, it was a paradise with all the trimmings. After the big one a few years ago, all of a sudden, the planet Pagama reformed, and we few survivors began our trek back home.

The snow vehicle bounced all over the jagged terrain, tossing him around. Broken ice pillars pierced the hull as air began to seep in. As it did, the driver heard a loud, high-pitched screeching. His eyes were nervous as he looked at his meters and gauges.

Looking around and breathing hard, he said, "It's coming! Crap! Crap! Come on!" His hands were shaking. "Move please! Please move!" he begged, shaking even more.

He hit the ignition, starting the vehicle. He was relieved it started as he continued on into the bone-chilling night.

Checkpoint. I have to rendezvous with everyone quickly. I have to keep going; maybe, just maybe, there are others left. There just have to be. It has to be. His eyes felt heavy.

*   *   *

Long ago, near an orbital station close to the eastern universe

Cosrack shouted in excitement, "Help! Look! Look!"

Ooka responded, "What in all Sam hill is going on?" Shocked, he dropped his coffee.

*   *   *

At the earth palace, Shine Shine . . .

Areesha called, "Father, Outpost Shine, near the eastern universe, has found something rather peculiar."

"What is it? A rock?" Maximus retorted in irritation.

King Silvair, the emperor of all the Shine Alliance and husband to Lynn, said, "Maximus, stop it. That's totally uncalled for . . . It's impossible. How can that be? Are my eyes playing tricks on me?"

A huge view screen showed the planet Pagama. It had somehow reformed itself and now existed once more. An expedition team was soon dispatched and headed off for the western universe.

Captain Elhuck announced, "We are going home, everyone."

Elder Zorse asked, "How did our home come back, and why? The *One* fought and cleansed the western universe years ago, ending the war and our enslavement. The savior vanished, and evil ceased to appear any longer."

Shahala added, "Soon, all of the Pagama refugees will return home. Praise be to the savior!"

Elder Zorse said, "Then our lord of the Pagama people will soon arise as well. He will lead us to an endless salvation. If the *One* had not vanished, he would be our leader and king now."

That is how it all started. The elder said, "Salvation," How wrong . . . how wrong he was . . . maybe.

*   *   *

Days earlier . . .

CHRONICLE LOG

ICE CITADEL

FIFTY-THREE DROP TEAMS FELL FROM THE STARS AND LANDED ON THE PLANET'S SURFACE. IT WAS A VIRGIN WORLD TO THEM, CLEAN AND UNTOUCHED. WHO KNEW WHAT SECRETS IT HELD? ALL THEY KNEW AND FELT WAS THAT THEY HAD COME HOME, AND A SENSE OF RELIEF FELL OVER THEM ALL.

CORSX SAID, "THIS IS SHINE EXPEDITION TEAM ICE RECON. WE ARE CIRCLING THE AREA AND MAKING A DROP ZONE. WE CAN SEE THE TERRAIN; IT APPEARS TO BE SIMILAR TO EARTH'S."

IGGIOMO ADDED, "BUT WE'VE ENCOUNTERED A HUGE ICE SPHERE. THE ANIMALS ARE FROZEN DEAD. I'M NOT TALKING ABOUT FROZEN LIKE IN THE FRIDGE; I'M TALKING ABOUT FROZEN AS IN IF YOU TOUCH THEM, THEY'LL CRUMBLE."

CORSX SAID, "WE'RE GOING IN TO INVESTIGATE. I HOPE WE HAVEN'T BITTEN OFF MORE THAN WE CAN CHEW ON THIS ONE."

* * *

MEANWHILE, ON THE SHIP ABOVE THE PLANET . . .

ADMIRAL SARAYANA YUKI SAID, "DO YOU HAVE A FEELING THAT SOMETHING IS WRONG—NOT DEADLY WRONG BUT DEATHLY WRONG?"

A SOLDIER RESPONDED, "WELL, MA'AM, IF I MAY SPEAK FREELY?"

* * *

DOWN ON THE PLANET . . .

"SO THIS IS IT, HUH? YOU MIGHT NOT COME BACK FROM THIS ONE, CORSX. CAN I HAVE YER STASH OF GURNAR ALE?" SAID IGGIOMO, GRINNING. "HEY, BROTHER, LOOK: YOU DO WHAT YOU GOT TO DO AND BRING YER SORRY TAIL BACK HERE, YOU HEAR ME? HOPEFULLY, IT'S JUST BAD MOJO VIBES AND NOTHING ELSE, RIGHT?"

CORSX REPLIED, "WE'RE MAPPERS THROUGH AND THROUGH. THIS IS OUR LIVES." HE OPENED HIS POCKET WATCH AND LOOKED AT IT.

ALL OF A SUDDEN, THE SNOW TERRAIN VEHICLE PULLED UP.

CORSX SAID TO THE DRIVER, "WHERE'D YOUR TEAM LAND, BURN?"

BURN, IN HIS COOL COUNTRY VOICE, REPLIED, "NEAR THE ICE SEA . . . CORSX, YOU DON'T HAVE TO SAY ANYTHING, OLD

PAL. I KNOW WHAT CRAZY THING YOU COOKED UP. I ALREADY KNOW YA GONNA HEAD IN THAT THING ALL ALONE, RIGHT? WELL, THAT BIG OLD SPHERE GOT OUR NAMES ON IT. HEY, I WAS JUST OUT ON RECON AND GOT LOST. THAT'S ALL." HE LAUGHED. "BESIDES, I'M NOT CUT OUT FOR HAULING SUPPLIES ANYHOW."

"I GOT MY SNOWSHOES AND MY SUPPLIES; I'M HEADED IN," SAID CORSX.

BURN SAID, "HOP ON. I'M HEADED IN WIT' YA. HANG ON, BUDDY."

CORSX ASKED, "YOUR TEAMS NEAR THE ICE SEA. DO YOU THINK THAT'S WHERE ALL THIS WATER CAME FROM TO FORM THIS HUGE ICE SPHERE, BURN?"

"I CAN'T HEAR YA. THE ENGINE'S ROAR IS TOO LOUD. HERE WE GO!" BURN SHOUTED, EXCITED AND FULL OF JOY.

BURN SWITCHED OUT THE THRUSTERS TO BLAST OFF INTO THE ICE SPHERE. HE WAS EXCITED AND PUMPED FOR THE ADVENTURE AND MYSTERY TO COME.

"WOO-HOO! YEAH! THIS IS THE LIFE," BURN SHOUTED. "AIR IN YER FACE AND MYSTERY AHEAD! THIS IS WHAT IT MEANS TO BE A MAPPER. LET'S RIDE!"

THE THRUSTERS OPENED TO GO FULL POWER AS THE SPEED GAUGE READ 1,010 MILES PER HOUR. CORSX WAS HOLDING ON FROM THE BACK USING HIS MAGNET LOCK RUNES, WHICH ANCHORED HIS FEET. THE SNOW WAS BLINDING, AND THE DETECTOR WAS GUIDING THEM FORWARD. BURN WAS DODGING CREEKS AND CREVASSES.

"SEEMS LIKE NO END, CORSX," BURN SAID. "WE'VE BEEN RIDING FOR HOURS NOW. CAN'T TELL IF IT'S DAY OR NIGHT, AND LOOK, OUR WATCHES ARE GOING HAYWIRE. WHAT CAN YOU MAKE OF THIS, BUDDY?"

"THERE HAS TO BE AN END, BURN," CORSX SAID. "THERE HAS TO BE." HE SHIVERED.

THEY VANISHED INTO THE COLD, MURKY DEPTHS OF THE RUINS AS IT BEGINS TO GET DARKER AND DARKER, AS THEY GOT FARTHER ALONG, THEY BEGAN TO SEE SOMETHING.

* * *

MEANWHILE, ELSEWHERE . . .

A PERSON ON A MECHANICAL STEAM HORSE GALLOPED ACROSS THE SEEMINGLY PEACEFUL PRAIRIES OF NEO PAGAMA.

"WHOA THERE, CLANK KNEES . . . THIS IS CLOCKWORK KNIGHT HERE. I'VE ENTERED THE PRAIRIE LANDS. IT APPEARS PEACEFUL."

THE SHINE DECOR OPERATOR SAID, "OKAY, CLOCKWORK."

"WAIT! I SEE SOMETHING AHEAD," CLOCKWORK SAID, SHOCKED.

A HUGE SPHERE OF GREEN FOLIAGE EXTENDED FROM THE RUINS OF A VAST TEMPLE. NOTHING BUT LARGE, THICK VINES COULD BE SEEN FROM AFAR.

CLOCKWORK SAID, "HMMM . . . IT APPEARS A CHALLENGE AWAITS US, EH, CLANK KNEES?"

STEAM PUFFED FROM HIS MOUNT'S NOSE. CLANK KNEES REARED UP, READY TO CHARGE INTO THE UNKNOWN. JUST THEN, IN THE BUSHES, CLOCKWORK SAW A SHADOW MOVING BEHIND HIM. HE MOVED HIS HAND TOWARD HIS LANCE BLADE.

SAMANTHA CALLED OUT, "CLOCKWORK, WAIT FOR ME! THE TEAM IS BY A HUGE FIRE MOUNTAIN."

"SAMANTHA, DEAR CHILD," HE SAID, "MYSTERY CALLS, AND CLANK KNEES AND I SHALL ANSWER POST-HASTE." HIS TIN MUSTACHE WIGGLED.

"CHILD!?" SAMANTHA REPEATED AND PUFFED UP, HER EXPRESSION TURNED ANGRY. "WHO ARE YOU CALLING A CHILD? I'M ALMOST FIFTEEN. YOU NEED ME. WHAT IF YOU RUST OR SOMETHING? COME ON; I CAN BE A LOT OF HELP, HUH?" SHE GIGGLED.

"SURELY, YOU JEST, DEAR GIRL", HE SAID. "WELL THEN."

"WELL THEN," SHE SAID. "I GUESS WE'RE HEADED IN THERE. LAST ONE IN IS A ROTTEN EGG!" SHE GIGGLED AGAIN.

CLOCKWORK CALLED, "WAIT! WAIT! OH DEAR!"

SAMANTHA SAID, "HURRY UP, OR YOU'LL MISS THE ADVENTURE!"

SHE HOPPED UP ON CLANK KNEES, AND THEY TOOK OFF FOR THE FOREST STRONGHOLD.

BY THEN, THE SATELLITE WAS PICKING UP THE ICE CITADEL'S SIGNAL AND THE TWO ADVENTURERS INSIDE.

SAMANTHA'S LOG TO BE CONTINUED . . .

*   *   *

CORSX LOG RESTART . . .

"YEE-HAW! NOTHING LIKE THE WIND IN YER FACE TO WAKE YOU UP, EH, BUDDY?" SAID BURN.

"WE MADE IT! WE MADE IT! LOOK AHEAD; IT'S A HUGE ICE TEMPLE WITHIN THIS PLACE. IT'S AMAZING!" SAID CORSX.

"DO YOU SMELL THAT?" ASKED BURN. "IT'S ADVENTURE, CORSX. IT'S CALLING US BIG-TIME." HE HOWLED.

"I DIDN'T ASK YOU TO COME ALONG, YA KNOW," SAID CORSX.

BURN LAUGHED. "WHAT? CAN'T HEAR YA! ENGINES, REMEMBER." HE LAUGHED AND HOWLED AGAIN.

ALL OF A SUDDEN, LIZARDIANS SPRANG FORTH FROM THE FROZEN MIST AS THE SNOW VEHICLE PLOWED ON. THEY LUNGED FORTH, ATTACKING AND CHASING THE VEHICLE.

"LIZARDIANS!" SAID CORSX. "BUT HOW IS THAT EVEN POSSIBLE? BURN. BURN! THEY'RE EVERYWHERE! WHAT ARE WE GOING TO DO, MAN? YOU KNOW HOW HARD IT IS TO TAKE ONE OF THESE THINGS DOWN!"

"I SEE THEM! I SEE THEM!," SAID BURN. "THIS IS WHY I SIGNED UP FOR THIS." HE GRITTED HIS TEETH AND LAUGHED. "ALL RIGHT, CORSX, IT'S TIME TO USE THE MODIFICATIONS I PUT IN. THE SHINE DRIVE—I INSTALLED A MINI ONE. ALL RIGHT, HERE WE GO!" HE LAUGHED WITH EXCITEMENT.

"WHAT?" SHOUTED A SURPRISED CORSX. "THOSE AREN'T LIZARDIANS!"

THE ICEZARDIANS WERE JUMPING ALL OVER THE ICE WALLS. SOME APPEARED BEFORE THE SNOW VEHICLE. IT HIT THEM, BUT THEY TURNED INTO SNOW. THE TWO ADVENTURERS CONTINUED ON

WITHOUT STOPPING TO INVESTIGATE. ALL THAT COULD BE HEARD THROUGH THE WALLS WERE ROARS AND AN ENGINE. BURN AND CORSX ENTERED THE ICE TEMPLE, LEAVING THEIR REPTILIAN PURSUERS BEHIND. ALL OF A SUDDEN, THE STORM PICKED UP, AND THEY WERE SNOW BLIND. THE SNOW VEHICLE ENDED UP RAMMING THROUGH THE TEMPLE WALLS. THEY CONTINUED ON, AND THE FRONT BLADES BROKE OFF FROM THE GLAZED-OVER AND HARDENED ICE.

"DID YOU SEE THAT?" SAID BURN. "HANG ON, CORSX. YOU GOOD, BUDDY? SORRY 'BOUT ALL THE BUMPS AND STUFF."

CORSX REPLIED, "NO PROBLEM. WHATEVER IS IN HERE HAS TO BE DANGEROUS FOR IT TO HAVE TURNED ALL OF THIS INTO A FROZEN WASTELAND. THIS ICE IS SO THICK THE SUN CAN'T EVEN MELT IT. I CAN ONLY IMAGINE THAT IF WE GO ANY FARTHER IT IS GOING TO BE FAR WORSE."

"THE ENGINE'S BEGINNING TO DIE," SAID BURN. "IT'S TOO DARN COLD. SHOOT! COME ON, BABY! YOU CAN DO IT. HANG IN THERE!"

BURN HIT THE PEDAL, RESTARTING THE ENGINE. THE ENGINE ROARED, AND THE SNOW VEHICLE THUNDERED ON. THE SNOW VEIL LIFTED, AND ONLY COLD DARKNESS COULD BE SEEN. BURN USED THE RADAR WHILE CORSX USED HIS NIGHT-VISION GOGGLES TO LOOK AROUND.

"BURN, HIT THE LIGHTS! I DON'T LIKE THIS." UP SO FAR AND NO SOUND; IT'S TOO QUIET.

BURN TURNED ON THE LIGHTS. AS THEY KEPT MOVING, THEY SOON SAW SNOW FLURRIES. THEN, FROM THE COLD SHADOWS . . .

CORSX SHOUTED, "BURN! ICEZARDIANS!"

"I'M ON IT!" SAID BURN. "WHOA! YOU HAD TIME TO RENAME THEM?"

THE ICEZARDIANS RAMMED THE VEHICLE, KNOCKING IT OFF COURSE AND OVER AN ICE-COVERED GUARDRAIL. THEY WERE HURLED DEEP INTO AN AREA FULL OF JAGGED ICE. IT TUMBLED TO THE BOTTOM AS CORSX'S BODY FIELD ACTIVATED TO PROTECT HIS BODY FROM IMPACT DAMAGE.

"YOU ALL RIGHT, BURN?" CORSX CALLED. "GOOD THING I HAD THESE MAGNET RUNES." HE LOOKED OVER THE SIDE AT THE ICE BELOW.

"YEAH," SAID BURN. "A FEW CUTS AND SCRAPES BUT ALL IN ALL NOT TOO BAD. THAT BODY FIELD YOU GOT SURE COMES IN HANDY, EH?" HE RUBBED HIS HEAD.

SUDDENLY, THE ICEZARDIANS REAPPEARED AND BEGAN BOMBARDING THE AREA WITH COLD FIRE. AS THE SHOTS HIT THE VEHICLE, IT BEGAN TO FREEZE. CORSX AND BURN HID BEHIND THE ICE VEHICLE. THEY WERE PINNED DOWN. FROM THE FRONT,

ICEZARDIANS APPEARED BEGINNING TO CHARGE THEIR BEAM MOUTH CANNONS.

CORSX AND BURN USED DETONATOR CHARGERS TO BLOW UP THE ICE TO FREE THE ICE VEHICLE. IT FELL ON ITS TREADS. BURN HOPPED IN AND OVERHEATED THE ENGINE. THE ICE VEHICLE RAN UP THE ICE WALL, SMASHING THE ICEZARDIANS, BUT THEY JUST BURST INTO SNOW. MORE ICEZARDIANS APPEARED, FOLLOWED BY EVEN MORE FROM THE VAST SNOW. BURN AND CORSX WASTED NO TIME MOVING FORWARD, BUT AS THEY DID, THEY NOTICED THAT THE REPTILES HAD STOPPED PURSUING THEM. CORSX TRIED TO FIGURE OUT WHY, BUT HE COULDN'T. THEY KEPT MOVING, AND A HUGE MURAL SOON CAME INTO SIGHT. THE MURAL HAD HOLES IN IT. AS THEY WENT FURTHER ALONG THE MURAL, ICE PILLARS EMERGED FROM THE HOLES AND SMASHED THE ICE VEHICLE. CORSX SAVED BURN JUST IN THE NICK OF TIME. HE LAID BURN DOWN AND BEGAN TO CHANNEL CHI ENERGY TO HIS HANDS TO BLOW THE TRAP TO BITS; WHEN THE SMOKE CLEARED, NOT A SCRATCH WAS ON IT. HE ATTACKED AGAIN; THIS TIME WITH A BARRAGE OF CHI ENERGY HITTING MULTIPLE POINTS BUT IT WAS USELESS.

"I KNEW IT," SAID CORSX. "THIS ICE IS TOO THICK FOR MY CHI ATTACKS . . . SOMETHING'S . . . SOMETHING'S . . . WHAT?" CORSX WAS SHOCKED BY WHAT HE SAW.

ICEZARDIANS MARCHED TOWARD THE TWO WEARY ADVENTURERS. THEY LOOKED AT EACH OTHER AND DECIDED TO CHARGE THE BEASTS HEAD-ON. CORSX RAN AND THEN JUMPED, FLYING THROUGH

THE AIR. HE HIT THE ICEZARDIAN, BUT ALL HE DID WAS END UP HURTING HIS HAND.

"MY HANDS!" CORSX SAID, LOOKING AT HIS BLEEDING HANDS.

"MY LEGS HURT; THEIR ICE BODIES ARE TOO THICK," SAID BURN.

THE BEASTS ATTACKED AS CORSX CHANNELED UP ENOUGH ENERGY TO CREATE A CHI BALL. HE SHOT IT TO HIT THEM DIRECTLY. THEY STILL DIDN'T EXPLODE OR EVEN CRUMBLE. SO HE TOOK FLIGHT AND RETURNED THE WAY THEY HAD COME.

"SO COLD," SAID CORSX, SHAKING. HIS TEETH CHATTERED. "BURN, YOU ALL RIGHT? TALK TO ME. CAN YOU HEAR ME?"

BURN HAD A FEVER AND WAS UNCONSCIOUS.

SOON, SOMETHING STRANGE BEGAN TO HAPPEN.

KRYONDONNA SAID, "YOUR FROZEN TREK INTO THE DARK ZONE HAS FAILED. YOUR POWER SIGNATURE HAS BEEN NOTICED. I SHALL AID YOU HOME."

SHE INSTANTLY TELEPORTED THEM, AND THEY WERE ABOARD THE SHINE DÉCOR.

GYOX, AN EXODONIAN WARRIOR, SAID, "SO, CORSX, MAPPER, YOU RETURN BATTERED AND BEATEN. AYE, WE FACED THE UNKNOWN, AND WE TOO HAVE RETURNED THANKS TO KRYONDONNA."

CORSX AND BURN WERE IN A RUNE CLARE, A SPECIAL FIELD THAT HEALED THE MIND, BODY, AND SOUL.

*   *   *

IN THE QUARTERS OF ADMIRAL YURI . . .

ZORNOGOYA SAID, "WE HAVE DETERMINED THAT THIS OR THE PLACES ENCOUNTERED ALL OVER NEO PAGAMA HAVE HIGH ENERGY READINGS. THE ICE IS SO THICK THAT CHI-BASED ATTACKS DO NOT WORK. THIS, MY DEAR FRIENDS, IS GOING TO BE AN EVENTFUL MOMENT IN SCIENTIFIC HISTORY.

KRYONDONNA SAID, "DANGER. IT LURKS HERE ON THIS NEW PAGAMA. SOMETHING FROM DAYS OF OLD THAT ONCE EXISTED ON THE PAGAMA OF THE FIRST AGE SLEEPS."

"MYSTIC EVENTS ARE HERE, AND WE MUST CONTINUE TO INVESTIGATE," SAID ADMIRAL YUKI WITH A WORRIED LOOK.

CORSX LOG TO BE CONTINUED . . .

CHRONICLE LOG

Forest Stronghold

The orbital satellites stationed around the planet picked up another adventurer . . .

This time, it centered in on the green sphere area where Clockwork Knight and Samantha had traveled to.

Clockwork Knight said, "So this is the green sphere. Huge majestic vines as large as buildings have sprouted everywhere. Amazing, simply amazing, I must say."

"I'm astounded at such a marvelous sight. Wowsers, commowsers!" said Samantha.

Clockwork Knight and his trusty steed, Clank Knees, moved forward without hesitation. But as they did, the shadows moved among the dense, entangled green. Soon, they were surrounded by creatures called Jargollies, which were huge vine beasts. Their vines shot toward Clockwork Knight. Samantha jumped down and rolled out of the way as Clank Knees's nose steamed and two latches opened to reveal flames. The beasts drew back and then took to the ceiling, climbing the entangled green.

Clockwork Knight used his spring arm. It began to turn and wind-up. When it was ready, he let loose, and it spun like a blade, ripping the vines to pieces. They fell shriveling up into husk, turning brown as they wilted. But the attack was not over yet. From the sky, more creatures came. Samantha caught them on her monster viewer. She could use this instrument to decode information about them. They were Gorbogos, or giant vine eyes. Vines shot out from them, bombarding the area.

As the vine onslaught came down, Clockwork Knight activated his knight-mode function. Clank Knees broke apart and melded with Clockwork Knight, forming his new armor becoming Clank Knees, the Gear Knight. Clank Knees unsheathed his mighty blade lance, known as the Grail Imperium. As soon as it was released, the beast fell and turned to husk. He sheathed the lance blade, and his mustache wiggled. He and Samantha continued on deeper into the unknown of the forest stronghold.

Clank Knees, the Gear Knight, said, "Samantha, you okay? Can you still function at minimal capacity? You seem hurt."

"I'm fine, just tired; that's all. Plus, all this humidity and sun is exhausting. Aren't you tired?" Samantha replied, wiping her head. She drank some water from her canteen.

Clank Knees, the Gear Knight, responded, "Not at all, milady, but if we must rest, then so shall it be. I was about to call Gearga. But if you insist you are fine, then I shall not."

Gearga were robot nurses. There were several series of this model ranging from surgical to war type. Clank Knees, the Gear Knight, picked Samantha up and carried her in his arms as they moved toward another room.

Samantha said, "Hmmm, it looks like this was or used to be some kind of water room, but where is the water?" She looked around to investigate, turning her head slowly.

Then all of a sudden as she looks about, something caught her eye. She told Clank Knees, the Gear Knight, to look in her direction. He saw the problem. They had to reconfigure the blocks in the room so it could start the flow once more. This would help them get to the other side in one piece. They went over to the mechanism. Clank Knees, the Gear Knight, had moved one piece before Samantha noticed a shadow was moving. Her monster decoder went off. When she opened it, a picture of a creature called a foxo foxy appeared. These were mischievous creatures that liked to play tricks. Every time Clank Knees, the Gear Knight, moved the blocks into the right place, they'd move them back. So Samantha and Clank Knees, the Gear knight, had to outfox the foxy. Samantha remembered that she had a few candy bits left in her adventure pack. She took them out, and the foxy looked at her approaching cautiously. While she did this, Clank Knees, the Gear knight, was able to finish the puzzle. The water came back, and they began to trek deeper into the unknown. Samantha and Clank Knees, the Gear Knight, made it to a huge room. Immediately after they entered, the door shut tight.

Clank Knees, the Gear Knight, said, "I think it's a trap, hmmm. Very well, a Mapper I will always be."

Samantha looked panicked. "I got a bad vibe about what's up ahead. But I joined the Mappers and I have to see it through."

Samantha's log to be continued . . .

CHRONICLE LOG

SILENT SANDS

THE DESERT IS AN UNFORGIVING PLACE OF SOLITUDE, AND THOSE WHO DARE IGNORE ITS MOST TREACHEROUS WARNINGS SUFFER ITS INTENSE AND HORRID JUDGMENT.

THE MOBILE TERRAIN TRANSPORT HURTLED ACROSS THE RUGGED SANDS. THIS WAS THE MAPPER DESERT TEAM. THEY WOULD TAKE ON DESERT-TYPE AREAS TOO DEADLY FOR REGULAR TEAMS.

RELSE SAID, "NOTHING LIKE IT, EH? MAPPER LIFE, I MEAN." HE RESUMED HUMMING A CHEERFUL TUNE.

WANSHREEMU, A MYSTIC ELDER, SAID, "YOU STILL HAVE YOUR JOY OF THIS, I SEE. WHETHER IT BE LIFE OR DEATH, EH, RELSE, NONE CAN ESCAPE THE POWER OF THE CONTRACT." THE ELDER WORE A DARK HOOD, SO THAT ONLY HIS RED EYES COULD BE SEEN.

ZORBOR, WIPING HIS HEAD, SAID, "IS THE AC ON? JEEZ, IT'S INSANE, MAN."

GOLROC SAID, "YOU SEE THE METER? IT MUST HAVE SOMETHING TO DO WITH THE PLANET ITSELF."

ZORBOR REPLIED, "IT'S FIVE HUNDRED DEGREES—WAIT . . . NO, IT'S BROKEN." HE LAUGHED.

"JUST HOW HOT IS THIS PLACE ANYHOW?" ASKED ANKHAIL. "MAN OH MAN. WE'VE BEEN ON PLANETS, BUT, SHEESH, NEVER LIKE THIS." HE POURED THE SWEAT OUT OF HIS BOOT.

THE M.T.T THUNDERED ACROSS THE SMOLDERING DESERT, AND THEN RELSE STOPPED THE VEHICLE. AS HE STOPPED, THE SAND FLEW EVERYWHERE.

RELSE SAID, "THIS IS IT, GUYS, THE END OF THE LINE. FROM HERE, YOU THREE BUMS GO ON FOOT."

"HEY, WHY I GOTTA GO?" ASKED ZORBOR IN AN UNPLEASANT TONE.

RELSE SMIRKED. "CAUSE I DRIVE THE TANK."

WANSHREEMU SAID, "WE MUST BE CAUTIOUS, OR WE MIGHT NOT RETURN THIS TIME."

"THIS ONE'S GOING TO BE A DOOZY, WORSE THAN THE OTHERS! YOU GUYS SURE YOU WANT TO GO?" ASKED RELSE.

WANSHREEMU INTERJECTED, "WE ARE MAPPERS; THIS IS WHAT WE DO. WE ARE TIED TO THE BOND OF THE CONTRACT AND MUST ABIDE BY IT."

"HUMPH, WHATEVER." RELSE FOLDED HIS HANDS BEHIND HIS HEAD.

AND SO THE THREE MAPPERS HEADED OUT INTO THE UNKNOWN OF THE TEMPLE OF THE SILENT SANDS. AS THEY MOVED FARTHER ALONG, THE HECTIC SANDSTORMS QUELLED THEIR AWESOME FURY, AND ONLY SILENCE COULD BE HEARD.

ZORBOR EXCLAIMED, "LOOK AT THE SIZE OF THAT DOOR! HOW CAN WE OPEN IT?"

ANKHAIL SAID, "THE HEAT APPEARS TO HAVE DIED DOWN, HMMMM."

GOLROC ADDED, "LOOK!, THE SUN IS GETTING CLOSER TO THE CRYSTAL OF THAT FALCON STATUE."

ALL OF A SUDDEN THE DOOR TURNED INTO SAND, LEAVING AN OPENING. AGAIN, NO SOUND WAS HEARD COMING FROM THE CRYPT. THE EXPLORERS MADE IT INSIDE THE HUMID DESERT STRONGHOLD. WHAT WONDROUS OR HORRID THINGS WOULD THEY ENCOUNTER.

ZORBOR HAD A PUZZLED LOOK ON HIS FACE. "HEY, LOOK! A RIVER OF SAND."

ANKHAIL ASKED, "DO YOU THINK THAT THESE ARE FROM THE PAGAMAS OF THE FIRST AGE? I'LL EXAMINE THE STONE."

"IF THEY ARE," SAID GOLROC, "THEN THE PLANET SOMEHOW REFORMED ITSELF AFTER THE GREAT APOCALYPSE THAT BEFELL THE WESTERN UNIVERSE."

ZORBOR SAID, "DON'T YOU MEAN WHEN THE SAVIOR APPEARED FROM THE HEAVENS AND VANQUISHED THE ECLIPSE LORD?"

"AS I SAID," SAID GOLROC, "BECAUSE OF THE APOCALYPSE, MANY THINGS WERE LOST. HOWEVER, WE ARE FREE."

"WHOA!" SAID ANKHAIL IN SURPRISE. "CHECK THIS OUT, FELLAS."

THEY ALL FOLLOWED THE RIVER OF SAND AND SAW THAT IT EMPTIED INTO A VAST OCEAN OF SAND. THE WINDOWS WERE SLANTED, AND SMALL RAYS OF SUNLIGHT SHOWED THROUGH.

GOLROC SAID, "HMM. THAT, UNLIKE WATER, IS SOMETHING WE CANNOT SWIM IN, AS IT WOULD APPEAR."

"I AGREE," SAID ANKHAIL.

ZORBOR SHRUGGED HIS SHOULDERS AND SMILED.

THERE WAS A LEDGE ABOVE THEM. ANKHAIL USED HIS GRAPPLER ARM AND PULLED HIMSELF UP, ONLY TO SEE MORE OF THE VAST OCEAN OF SILENT SAND.

ANKHAIL SAID, "IT APPEARS WE SHOULD CAMP OR SET UP A MARKER AT LEAST."

AFTER THEY SET UP CAMP, THEY BEGAN TO EXPLORE ON THEIR OWN.

ANKHAIL SAID, "THESE ANCIENT CARVINGS ARE ASTOUNDING; BEING A MAPPER HAS ITS DAYS, I SUPPOSE." HE CHUCKLED TO HIMSELF.

HE SAW SOMETHING OUT OF THE CORNER OF HIS EYE. IT APPEARED TO BE A CHILD OR RATHER . . .

"LOUISE, MY LOVE, HOW'D YOU GET HERE? I THOUGHT YOU WERE ON ASSIGNMENT?" HE SAID.

LOUISE APPROACHED HIM. SHE RUBBED HIS CHEEK AND THEN KISSED HIM SO VERY PASSIONATELY. HE PUSHED HER BACK. SHE HELD OUT HER HAND AND TURNED TO SAND. ANKHAIL GOT UP, STAGGERED AROUND THEN FELL.

"NO!" HE SAID. "THE CURSE OF THE SILENT SANDS IN THESE WRITINGS . . ." HE STOPPED TO COUGH. " . . . MUST HOLD A CURE. WAIT! NO!" HE WAS TURNING TO SAND. "SO THIS IS HOW I END MY TIME. GOOD LUCK, FELLOWS!"

THE WIND SILENTLY BLEW HIS DUST AWAY . . .

Golroc called out, "Ankhail, are you there? Zorbor, can you hear me?" He heard nothing but static.

Golroc ducked just in time as a claw emerged from the shadows.

"Aye, so I'm not alone, eh?" He felt himself sweat. "So be it then. Have at thee."

A sad voice said, "You who dare enter the silent sands shall too be claimed by them. Come unto us for all eternity."

Loud, angry voices joined the chorus, "Adventurers of youth who dare trespass on our graves, we the silent sands, shall consume you all!"

"Well," said Golroc, turning up his lip. "I'm a mapper through and through. We take on the toughest of all missions. We're the do-or-die squad. We've looked death in the eye and returned every time. But old death, ya see, he waits and laughs. He knows we will see him soon enough. I used to be a rescue-squad team member. But my squad died and I . . . I . . ." He hesitated. " . . . survived. Now I'm here, so . . ."

The sands began to shift and moan. From within them, skeleton pirates arose. They were the foolish ones who had sought the sands' mysterious treasures. Now, they guarded them and devoured

THE SOULS OF ANY WHO SOUGHT THEM. THE SKELETONS LOOKED AT HIM WITH THEIR DEAD EYES AND MOVED IN SLOWLY TO ATTACK. THEY BEGAN TO EDGE CLOSER AND CLOSER AS GOLROC PREPARED HIMSELF.

¡SO YOU WANT TO JUMP? THEN JUMP!~ HE TAUNTED IN A BOLD BUT FRIGHTENED VOICE. GOLROC~S BOLD AND SCARED VOICE CHALLENGED THE ONCOMING SKELETONS.

THE SKELETONS CHARGED, BEGINNING THEIR RUTHLESS ASSAULT AS GOLROC USED HIS POWER-UP TECHNIQUE, WHICH BOOSTS HIS STRENGTH. GOLROC ENGAGES THE SKELETONS FROM ABOVE, EVADING THEIR ATTACKS. THE MAPPER, GOLROC USED A FORCE-FIST TECHNIQUE; FORCE FIST COMPRESSED THE ENERGY OF THE FIST AND WRIST MUSCLES, BUILDING ENERGY AS THE FIST IS EXTENDED IN A PUNCHING MOTION. WHEN THIS HAPPENED, IT UNLEASHED A POWERFUL, INVISIBLE ENERGY WAVE. THE SKELETONS WERE PUMMELED, CRUMBLING TO BONES ONCE MORE BEFORE TURNING INTO SAND. GOLROC WAS SURROUNDED AS MORE SKELETONS APPEARED, THIS TIME SLASHING AT HIM WITH THEIR CUTLASSES. HE DODGED, LOSING WHISPS OF HIS HAIR. THE RUSTED, LETHAL BLADES CLASH AS THEY TRIED TO BEHEAD HIM. THE SKELETON PIRATES FINALLY TRAPPED GOLROC BETWEEN THEM AND TRIED TO STAB HIM. BUT HE CARTWHEELED OUT OF THE WAY, AND THEIR BLADES IMPALE EACH OTHER.

GOLROC QUICKLY USED FORCE FIST, TO DESTROY THEM. MORE SKELETON PIRATES ARISE AS HE CAUGHT HIS BREATH. GOLROC EXTENDED HIS HAND

AND USED A FORCE WAVE; AN INVISIBLE ENERGY WAVE HIT THE GROUP OF SKELETONS, TURNING THEM TO SAND. JUST AS GOLROC BREATHED A SIGH OF RELIEF, HE SAW THAT THE PIRATES WERE RISING UP ONCE MORE. NOW, THEY WERE POURING FORTH FROM THE CATACOMBS AND CRYPTS. THOUSANDS OF LOST SOULS ENSLAVED TO SERVE THE SILENT SANDS WERE RISING. WHAT LAY BENEATH THESE SANDS THAT MUST BE DEFENDED WITH ONE~S VERY OWN LIFE? GOLROC LOOKED ON AT THEIR VAST NUMBERS. HE RAN AND JUMPED, FLIPPING ONTO THE WALL. HE USED CHI RICOCHET. MOVING FROM WALL TO WALL, BOUNCING AND STRIKING THE SKELETONS. BUT AS HE SUSPECTED, THEY BEGAN TO RISE AGAIN. RUNNING OUT OF BOTH OPTIONS AND TIME, HE JUMPED UP, USING EMPEROR FLAME. THIS WAS A FIST-STYLE FIRE ATTACK. FLAMES IGNITED IN THE AIR BECAUSE OF THE PERSON~S ANGER OR WILL OF COURAGE AND THEN EXPLODED FROM THE HAND OR FIST. WHEN GOLROC USED THE TECHNIQUE, IT EXPLODED FROM HIS FIST WITH INTENSE FEROCITY, TURNING THE SAND TO GLASS. HE LANDED, FALLING. HE WAS TIRED BUT KNEW HE COULDN~T REST. NEXT, HE USED CHI SPRINT. THIS WAS ENERGY BUILT UP IN THE LEG MUSCLES TO MAKE A PERSON MOVE FASTER. HE VANISHED DEEPER INTO THE CATACOMBS OF THE SILENT SANDS.

GOLROC RAN THROUGH THE DIMLY LIT HALLS, SOON THE SHADOWS BEGIN TO STIR AND MOVE. GOLROC KEPT MOVING WHILE, AT THE SAME TIME TRYING TO CONTACT ZORBOR. BUT, ALAS, IT WAS NO USE. COULD THE SILENT SANDS HAVE CLAIMED ANOTHER SOUL?

GOLROC HEARD SINISTER LAUGHTER. "SO SOME FOOL DARES TO ENTER THE SANDS? SOON, LET THEM RELEASE THE LOCK AND FIND THE SO-CALLED SACRED TREASURE, THEN I WILL BE FREE TO PLUNDER PAGAMA FOR MY OWN ONCE MORE!" EVIL LAUGHTER FOLLOWED.

GOLROC SAID, "THOSE RUINS SAID, "BEWARE THE ONE WHO DWELLS IN THE DARK. THE SACRED LOCKS MUST NEVER BE BROKEN."

*　*　*

AS GOLROC MOVED THROUGH THE CATACOMBS, ZORBOR MADE IT TO A LONG BRIDGE, BENEATH WHICH WAS A BOTTOMLESS HOLE OF DARKNESS. HE BEGAN TO MOVE FORWARD AND SOON HEARD THE VOICES OF THE DEAD BEGINNING TO STIR AND SPEAK. ZORBOR STOPPED.

A VOICE, BONE-CHILLING TO THE SPINE, WARNED, "HEED THEE WELL, ADVENTURER OF THIS AGE. LET NOT YOUR EYES COVET JEWELS. TURN BACK, AND THY FREEDOM IS GRANTED."

ZORBOR ANSWERED IN A BRAVE BUT FRIGHTENED VOICE, "I AM A MAPPER, AN ADVENTURER. I AM AN ARCHEOLOGIST. THESE ANCIENT RUINS BECKON TO BE HEARD."

THE VOICE SAID, "SO THE WARNING YE NOT TAKE, EH? WELL, A PALE HORSE SHALL THEE VISIT."

THE BLACK SANDS STIRRED AND TREMBLED. FROM THE HATE-FILLED SOIL CAME A PALE SKELETAL HORSE, DECAYED WITH ITS BONES WORN AND BLEACHED. PALE HORSE MOVED SWIFTLY TOWARD ZORBOR. HE DODGED, MOVING BEHIND IT AS IT LOOKED AT HIM.

PALE HORSE'S MANE FIRE NEEDLE-LIKE HAIRS AT ZORBOR. HE MANAGED TO EVADE THEM AS HIS ARM GRAPPLE-HOOKED A LEDGE ON THE OTHER SIDE OF THE HUGE BLACK PIT. HE MANAGED TO PULL HIMSELF OVER AND ESCAPE FOR NOW. A SENSE OF RELIEF CAME OVER HIM; HE THOUGHT HE WAS SAFE BUT SAW THE PALE HORSE DETACH ITS BODY FROM THE BLACK SANDS AND BEGIN TO RUN ON THE AIR ITSELF. ZORBOR TRIPPED OVER HIS OWN FEET AS HE RAN, WITHOUT LOOKING BACK. PALE HORSE GALLOPED TO END ZORBOR'S LIFE BUT FROM AN UNKNOWN SOURCE, A HUGE ENERGY BLAST HIT THE GHASTLY BEAST, SENDING IT FALLING INTO THE DARK DEPTHS.

DOWN IN THE PIT . . .

PALE HORSE CALLED IN A HORRIBLE, ANGRY VOICE, "YOU DARE CHALLENGE ME. I AM AN END BEAST GUARDIAN OF OLD. FOOLISH SORCERER, COME AND BE DEFEATED AT THINE OWN RISK."

"YES, I DARE!" REPLIED A SINISTER SKELETON VOICE. "ONCE THAT FOOL BREAKS THE SEAL, I WILL BE FREE FROM THE SILENT SANDS." ZORBOR HEARD ITS EVIL LAUGHTER.

PALE HORSE SAID, "I AM PALE HORSE, GUARDIAN OF OLD. YOU DARE TO DEFY THE DIVINE JUDGMENT THAT HATH BEEN SENT UPON THEE, SKULL SORCERER? THOU THINK THY POWER IS GREAT ENOUGH TO TOPPLE ME?"

SKULL SORCERER GRAIL RA RESPONDED, "I AM GRAIL RA, THE SKULL SORCERER, AND SOON, I WILL BE FREED." HE WAS WALKING AND TALKING, WATCHING HIS EVERY MOVE.

"TO RISE AGAINST THE SKELETON KING IS ETERNAL SUFFERING AS YE HAVE ENDURED, SORCERER," SAID PALE HORSE.

GRAIL RA LAUGHED EVILLY. "SOON, PALE HORSE, I WILL BE FREED. FREE TO CLAIM THE GOD'S POWER AND THEN THIS WORLD. SOON, THE SKELETON KING WILL BOW TO ME. SO BE GONE FROM MY SIGHT, USELESS RELIC."

PALE HORSE'S ENERGY IGNITED INTO FURY AS HORRIBLE FLAMES SURROUNDED THE AREA. BLACK, CRIMSON, RED FLAMES BURNED EVERYTHING THEY TOUCHED. GRAIL RA LOOKED ON WITH CAUTION NOT UNDERESTIMATING THE OLD BEAST FROM A FORGOTTEN AGE.

PALE HORSE SAID, "NOT SO EASY, SO IT WOULD SEEM, SORCERER. FIRST, TRY AND BEST ME, AN END BEAST!"

GRAIL RA LAUGHED ARROGANTLY AND SAID, "IF IT'S AN END YOU SEEK, SO BE IT."

LIGHT COULD BE SEEN FROM THE HOLE WITH PATCHES HERE AND THERE. ZORBOR SAW FLASHES OF LIGHT BUT CONTINUED ON TO THE MAIN TREASURE ROOM OF THE SILENT SANDS. HE RAN ONWARD AS THE FLOOR AHEAD BEGAN TO VANISH. ZORBOR STOPPED FOR A MOMENT THEN CONTINUED ON ANYWAY. AN IMAGE CAME TO HIS MIND; HE SAW THE HIEROGLYPHICS. THEY SAID, "CONTINUE ON, YE OF FAITH. SEEK WHAT CANNOT BE SOUGHT. SOUGHT WHAT CANNOT BE. BLOOD SOAKED IN LIFE. FAITH TOWARD THE EYE OF EYES." HE STEPPED FORWARD AND FELL INTO A SUBSPACE POCKET, A PLACE BETWEEN THE TEMPLE AND THE OUTSIDE WORLD. AT LAST, ZORBOR MADE IT TO THE TREASURE ROOM. IT GLISTENED SO BEAUTIFULLY. HE WAS AMAZED AND ASTOUNDED.

"SO MUCH TREASURE! IF ONLY THE OTHERS COULD SEE THIS! BUT THAT'S NOT WHY I'M HERE," HE SAID.

A LIGHT SHONE BRIGHTLY AS IF CALLING OUT TO HIM. THERE, BEFORE HIS EYES, WAS THE SACRED TREASURE OF THE SILENT SANDS.

A YELLOWISH GEM SHINED WITH A MAGNIFICENT LIGHT, ALMOST LIKE A HIDDEN POWER, WAITING FOR ZORBOR.

HE WONDERED WHAT WOULD HAPPEN IF ANYTHING WERE TO BE MOVED OUT OF PLACE. HE GRASPED THE GEM, AND A SURGE THUNDERED THROUGHOUT THE TEMPLE OF THE SILENT SANDS. ALL OF A SUDDEN, HE HEARD A BONE-CHILLING LAUGH.

ZORBOR COMMANDED, "SILENCE, ALL YE AILING SPIRITS. I HAVE FOUND ONE OF THE KING'S JEWELS NEEDED TO ASCEND THE THRONE OF PAGAMA. I WILL FIND THEM ALL AND AWAKEN PAGAMA, USHERING IN A NEW AND GRAND AGE OF GREATNESS. LET THIS MARK MY FIRST DEED AS TRIUMPHANT."

THERE WAS CLAPPING. "SO . . . YOU HOPE TO BECOME AN ALL-POWERFUL KING, EH?" HE HEARD LAUGHTER.

AN ENERGY BLAST HIT ZORBOR, KNOCKING HIM OVER THE ALTAR. THE GEM FELL OUT OF HIS HAND. HE TRIED TO GET UP, BUT THE BLACK ENERGY SQUEEZED HIM TIGHTER.

"I AM GRAIL RA, THE SKULL SORCERER. YOU HAVE RELEASED ME! I WAS ALMOST DEVOURED BY THAT OLD TITAN BEAST BUT THANKS TO YOU" HE LAUGHED. "NOW THIS GEM IS MINE!" THERE WAS MORE LOUD LAUGHTER.

ZORBOR FLOATED TO THE SKULL SORCERER AS HE MOTIONED WITH HIS HAND. WHEN HE TOUCHED ZORBOR'S HEAD, THE MAPPER BEGAN TO SCREAM IN HORROR AND AGONY.

* * *

ELSEWHERE . . .

GOLROC SAID, "WHAT THE . . . ?" HE WAS SHOCKED AND CONFUSED.

THE VOICE SAID, "THE SEAL HATH BEEN BROKEN AND HORRORS UNLEASHED FROM DAYS OF OLD. AGONY, PAIN, DARKNESS, NOW HENCE YE HAVE HEARD."

THE TEMPLE OF THE SILENT SANDS BEGAN TO SINK AND IMPLODE, TRAPPING ANYONE STILL IN THERE. GOLROC HAD NO TIME TO LOSE. SAND BEGAN POURING IN FROM EVERYWHERE AS HE RAN. THE SKELETON BEAST APPEARED ALONG WITH THE SAND BEAST.

GOLROC SCREAMED, "NO!"

*   *   *

DAYS LATER . . .

THE SEARCH-AND-RESCUE PILOT SAID, "ROGER; I'VE FOUND A SURVIVOR."

THE PILOT LANDED THE RESCUE CRAFT.

"HEY, MAN, WHERE YOU BEEN?" ASKED THE PILOT. "YOU LOOK EXHAUSTED."

ZORBOR GROANED AND FELL INTO THE SAND FACE-FIRST, WHERE HE LAY, NOT MOVING.

THE PILOT SAID INTO HIS RADIO, "MED UNIT REQUESTED, MED UNIT FOR ZORBOR MAPPER'S DEATH CREW."

MAPPER'S LOG TO BE CONTINUED . . .

CHRONICLE LOG

PAGAMA CASTLE

HAGGLESBEE'S LOG BEGINS . . .

HE WAS OUT FLYING THE SKY STREAM OF THE PLANET. HE COULD NOT BELIEVE HOW QUIET AND BEAUTIFUL IT WAS IN THE SKY; IT WAS SO AMAZING.

AS HE WAS FLYING, ALL OF A SUDDEN, A GIANT, SWIRLING CLOUD REVEALED TO HIM A CASTLE AMONG THE MAJESTIC BLUE.

HAGGLESBEE SAID, "IT'S AS IF IT WERE CALLING ME TO IT."

HE FLEW IN AS THE DRAWBRIDGE WAS LOWERING. HE LANDED AND THEN DISEMBARKED. HE WALKED INTO THE CASTLE. IT WAS TOO OVERWHELMING AS AN AURA FLUSHED INTO HIS BODY, TELLING HIM SOMETHING. IT BEGAN TO READ HIM AND TOLD HIM THAT HE WAS HOME. THOSE WORDS BEGAN TO FLOW INTO HIM. HE THOUGHT THAT HE MIGHT KNOW THEM.

HAGGLESBEE SAID, "THE LORD OF THE PAGAMA PEOPLE, ONLY THE STRONGEST OF THE PAGAMA MAY SEEK NOBILITY. TO CLAIM THEY ARE STRONGER THAN THE OLD LORD—HE

WHO IS PAGA-JIN. THE ANCIENT LANGUAGE SPEAKS OF A DARK ONE WHO WAS IMPRISONED. HE ASCENDED BUT WANTED THE DARK TO RULE ON HIGH FOR ALL ETERNITY; THUS, THE SHADOW REALM WAS BORN. NOW HE WHO BECAME LORD OF THE PAGAMA HAD WISE COUNCIL AND THROUGH HARSH BATTLE WITH THE FORCES OF THE NIGHT WAS ABLE TO VANQUISH THE NIGHTMARES OF OLD. THE POWER OF THE ELDERS AIDED HE WHO WAS HIM. NOW, AN EVIL HATH BEEN LET LOOSE. NOW A NEW TALE UNFOLDS."

A NEO LEGEND . . .

AS HAGGLESBEE WALKED THE HALLS OF THE CASTLE, HE MARVELED AT THE ARCHITECTURE. AS HE GOT CLOSER AND CLOSER TO THE END OF THE HALLWAY, HE SAW LIGHT AND WITHIN THE LIGHT A FIGURE.

"I THOUGHT YOU WERE A STATUE," HAGGLESBEE SAID.

"HO THERE, TRAVELER. WHO ARE THEE?" THE FIGURE ASKED.

"I'M A PAGAMA WHO HAS RETURNED TO RECLAIM HIS BIRTHRIGHT." HAGGLESBEE ANSWERED HIM WITH PRIDE IN HIS VOICE

"I AM THE CARETAKER HERE WAITING FOR THE ONE, THE LEADER OF ALL PAGAMA PEOPLE. COME WALK WITH ME."

THEY WALKED THE HALLS OF THE CASTLE AND HOLD CONVERSATION. THE DAY TURNED TO NIGHT.

HAGGLESBEE SAID, "I'VE COME HERE WITH A PAGAMA TEAM FROM THE EARTH COLONIES. AFTER WE SEND SURVEYS BACK, WE'LL BEGIN TO REPOPULATE AND REBUILD."

THE CARETAKER CHUCKLED. "WE ARE NOTHING WITHOUT OUR LEADER. AS IT IS WRITTEN IN THE TABLETS OF THE ELDERS AND ETCHED IN THE STONES, ONLY THE ONE WHO WIELDS THE BLADE AND CONQUERS THE TRIALS MAY SEEK THE THRONE OF THE KING TO ASCEND, FOR HE HATH THE COURAGE AND UNDERSTANDING TO LEAD OUR PEOPLE TO THE PLATINUM AGE, AN AGE SO GLORIOUS NO EVIL SHALL STAIN IT."

"THE TRIALS?" SAID HAGGLESBEE, RUBBING HIS CHIN.

THE CARETAKER EXPLAINED, "YES, FIVE PLACES OF SACRED POWER STAND ON THIS PAGAMA SOIL. FIVE SACRED TREASURES EXIST WITHIN THESE STRUCTURES TO TEST THE MANTLE OF THOSE WHO WOULD DARE BE KING OR DARE TRY TO CLAIM THE TITLE OF KING. ONE HAS ALREADY BEEN FOUND, MY YOUNG TRAVELER. THERE IS SOMEONE ELSE WHO SEEKS THE THRONE OF PAGAMA. COME; I MUST SHOW YOU SOMETHING."

HAGGLESBEE FOLLOWED THE OLD MAN, WHO LED HIM TO A ROOM THAT LOOKED LIKE A PLACE FIT FOR ROYALTY. HAGGLESBEE WALKED FORWARD AND THEN HIT A BARRIER.

"WHAT THE . . . ? THIS IS A SHIELD OF SOME KIND." SAID HAGGLESBEE

THE CARETAKER SAID, "YES, IT IS. THIS IS THE KING'S ROAD; NONE MAY ENTER THIS HOLY GROUND SAVE THE ONE TRUE KING. IT IS WRITTEN THAT TO UNLOCK THE BARRIER, THE ONE MUST OBTAIN ALL FIVE SACRED TREASURES AND THEN SIT UPON THE KING'S THRONE TO BE JUDGED AND DEEMED WORTHY."

"TO BE KING AND DEEMED WORTHY," HAGGLESBEE SAID. "THE TRIALS CALL TO ME SINCE ONE HAS ALREADY BEEN FOUND? A DARKNESS IS WAITING TO REACH OUT ITS HAND ONCE MORE TO CLAIM ALL OF PAGAMA. ALL I KNOW IS . . . IS . . . I'M HOME, AND THIS TIME, NO ONE'S GOING TO TAKE THAT AWAY FROM ME."

THE OLD MAN SMILED AS HAGGLESBEE LEFT THE CASTLE.

HAGGLESBEE TOOK OFF AND VANISHED INTO THE NIGHT. WHO KNOWS WHERE HIS DESTINATION LIES?

HAGGLESBEE'S LOG TO BE CONTINUED . . .

CHRONICLE LOG

Forest Stronghold

Continued

Samantha's log restart . . .

Beasts burst forth from the lush greenery. Huge human shaped vine creatures began their onslaught. These vine warriors were moving rapidly toward Clockwork Knight, who had transformed back.

Clockwork Knight said, "Onward, Clank Knees. We're almost there. We can outrun them. These vines are getting huge. We must be nearing the source. Hang on, Samantha."

Clockwork Knight then saw the shadows shift, from the green comes huge vine beasts called Vinezardians that were attacking furiously. Two beasts missed him, however, Clockwork Knight is knocked off from his trusted steed, Clank Knees. Clank Knees flees with Samantha on his back as more Vinezardians appeared from the ground. They damaged Clank Knees causing Samantha to fall and hurt herself. Clank Knees's begins to stagger; gears and oil were spilling everywhere.

Clockwork got up and unsheathed his lance blade—the Grail Imperium. Clockwork charges his foes, throwing his lance and lopped off the Vinezardian's head. As one fell, five more appeared, Clockwork Knight leapt over them and hefted his lance blade as he turned around and chopped off their legs. The plant like creatures, roots began to regrow, so he used his rocket-fist attack to blast them to pieces. The vined beasts fall but rise again, this time dividing themselves into more groups as more and more crawled forth. Clockwork Knight ran, twirling the blade, which was attached to his arm. He did devastating damage; as the beasts fell and did not rise again. Next, his heart core ignited, and the lance blade turned to flames of courage, resulting in a backlash of energy. The Vinezardians fell into husk, he ran into the beasts as they began their onslaught. Not showing an ounce of fear, he fought onward. Vines appeared out of their claws like whips, which were covered in a corrosive poison. Clockwork dodges the assault and uses Vulcan lance barrage: a fire-based attack that shot out multiple flame-blade lances that had a two-second time limit before they exploded. As he went further into the Green, more poured out.

Clockwork Knight said, "Exhaust port open; Egan charge."

The Egan charge expels, releasing a huge burst of electric power that filled the area, frying anything in the way. After unleashing the powerful attack, all the remains were burned to husks with scorched vines.

Clank Knees limped over to Clockwork Knight along with Samantha.

Clockwork Knight said, "Aye, my friend, thank you for protecting her. Now, we are able to ride on? Can you go on, my old steed?"

Clank Knees reared up, ready to go. Clockwork Knight and Samantha saddled up; as they kept moving, the light they saw began to blind them. Who knows what perils await our knight, his steed, and the little girl? Have they finally reached the end of the forest stronghold? After defeating multiple hoards of creatures, Clockwork Knight and his team continued deeper into the green stronghold's depths, even though they were both damaged. Clank Knees gallops at top speed, putting strain on his legs' servos, which were almost broken. Clockwork Knight was slashed across his chest gears, and his Imperium armor was broken. They kept getting closer to the light; it got brighter and soon the area began to change from vines and green to ruins of light. The sun was shining, but the area was hot and humid. They saw water, but as it hit the ground, it was evaporating. The ground was not cracked. It still retained some moss wrapped around the ruins of the stone statues.

Samantha wiped her head and opened her jacket. "Clockwork, do you see that? It's so bright my scanner goggles tell me it's a jewel. Look out!" she shouted.

As they ran through the halls, Vinezardians were again arising, but these were bigger and stronger than the others. Clockwork Knight charged at full speed as they tried to block his way. The beasts pounced with their fangs and claws dripping with poison. They moved at uncanny speeds, but Clockwork hurled his Shield of the Hero at them. It sliced their heads off as their speed worked to his advantage; at the same time, he pole-vaulted over them and Clank Knees ran on with Samantha. While still in the air, the lance blade extended, hitting the Vinezardians. Runes on the lance then lit up. The Pyrona flare was activated, shooting flames out in eight directions. Almost all the beasts were obliterated. The one remaining charged at him, but Clank Knees just then returned with Samantha. Clank Knees reared up, using his hoof missiles destroying the beast.

Samantha smiled and said, "What? I knew you needed my help." She giggled.

The wounded Mappers continued on, and soon, they could see an altar of light. They approached the altar of light very cautiously. Clockwork Knight wiggled his mustache looking around with a serious but cheerful face. They moved slowly, admiring the architecture and ruins. They found it odd that with all the light, the area was not heated at all.

Clockwork Knight said, "Aye, Clank Knees, who's to know how many adventurers of our own have perished? We have not seen any bones. Nay, maybe they returned to the dirt and cosmos from which they came."

Clank Knees continued on and suddenly, a huge shadow appeared to smash the noble steed to bits. Clockwork grabbed Samantha before they could be squished as well. As they got up, what stood before them was a beast that he knew all too well. It was a Dragongonian. This beast looked as if it had seen many a battle and many wars by the scars that lay upon its brow and all over its body. The beast roared in dominance as if saying, "Who are you to dare to enter my sacred grounds?"

Clockwork Knight rose up, unsheathing his lance blade, the Grail Imperium. He retrieved his Helmet of the Forlorn. Samantha was shaking with fright. She looked at Clockwork and soon felt a sense of confidence come over her.

Clockwork Knight said to the beast, "So ye be our foe. A mighty judgment awaits all those who try claiming this ominous treasure. So be it if this be my end; shall it be glorious." He shouted to the girl, "Come, Samantha; into battle, we go!"

The beast took flight, roaring as Clockwork Knight ran at it. Using the Catavault Lance, he hurled himself into the air toward the Dragongonian. The beast saw it and fires off one giant burst of light flames, one after the other. One was headed directly in Samantha's path. She froze in terror. Clockwork's feet rollers activated in time, and he grabbed her from the jaws of danger, but the bombardment continued. Clockwork Knight used his Hero Shield to block the flames that lay across the ground. They were thrown back near the altar where Samantha saw the jewel of light. She ran for it, but then the beast appeared with phantom speed. The movement of this huge beast creates a sweeping gust knocking her back. She rolled down the altar steps. Clockwork Knight saw she was in danger and acted. The Dragongonian flew to the top of the room where a hole opened. From there, the sun covered the entire room. The beast could absorb the sun. They couldn't see what the beast was doing, but Clockwork had an idea of what was going to happen.

A huge beam of intense light rained down on them as they began to flee. They dodged debris as, the ground explodes around them. From the smoke cover, the beast flew in, again firing flames from its mouth. These flames were so hot they were melting the ruins, and the air was evaporating, into deadly vapors. Samantha began to feel dizzy, as she leaned on Clockwork Knight. He opened his chest compartment using his oxygen mask on her. He gave her his Hero pendant, which set up a shield when something came into contact with it. As he turned around, his mustache wiggled.

Clockwork Knight charged in using the Vault Lance. The lance extended, almost stabbing the beast, but it only scraped its scales. Next, he climbed the walls by punching into them. The Dragongonian saw him and attacked, using light shards from its wings. They stuck into the wall as Clockwork Knight fell. The beast flew in, and its feet dug into the ground as it tried to pick up Clockwork Knight. He used the lance blade, slicing at the beast; however, no blood came out. The beast kicked him across the room into the wall. He tried to get up, but his leg joints began to fall apart, and are becoming stiff. He quickly looked around, but the beast was nowhere in sight. From the air, a Dragongonian hand grabbed him and flung him into the outside chambers. The beast began smashing the area. Clockwork Knight was surviving—but barely. From the smoke and debris, the lance blade shot off the Vulcan Storm, a huge spiral of flame and wind with energy attached to it. The Dragongonian was wounded falling to the ground groaning. Clockwork ran as best he could; using the Pole-Vault Lance, he took to the sky. While in the air, he ejected his hand and inserted the Grail Imperium. He moved with alarming speed, coming at the wounded beast. The beast was not unconscious at all, and it saw Clockwork Knight from the corner of its eye. As he came down, it flipped back, slapping him with its tail. He spiraled through the air uncontrollably. The beast looked at him as if to say, "I have you now." It fired off its light-beam cannon from its mouth. Clockwork saw it as his calf boosters ignited. He spun through the air as the beam hit. The lance blade was turning so fast in midair that he was plowing through it. He almost beheaded the beast, but the Dragongonian flew up, opening its mouth then getting ready to go for the kill.

The energy beam left Clockwork smoking and burned while the armor he wore was blackened and nearly destroyed. Clockwork struggled to stand up as his servos and gears gave out on him. The mighty Dragongonian flew up. Samantha tried to get to the gem, but the vapors were becoming too strong as they thickened around the altar.

Clockwork Knight said, "So 'tis the conclusion here and now, eh, beast? Well then, have at thee!" I must hurry; Samantha is flesh and blood while I am not. I must end this fight for her sake, he thought.

The Dragongonian of light flew up, its light fangs burning with full cosmic malice. It was ready to end the knight's life in an instant. It watched him, moving slowly. Clockwork Knight, with the Grail Imperium in hand, used a forbidden and ancient skill. He uttered a few words, then the lance glowed with such radiance and ominous power; Runes never seen before appeared.

Clockwork Knight said, "Alrus legende."

They collided, and the lance blade struck the beast through the mouth to the back of its brain, or rather its core membrane. The beast's entire head was removed. The Dragongonian fell into a pit alongside the jewel altar. Clockwork Knight, badly damaged, had stuck the lance into the wall as he fell. It began scraping down the side as he managed to slow himself down. He climbed up with the remaining power he had, making it out of the hole. He then walked pass the toxic vapors. Just as Clockwork Knight was about to get the jewel, the headless beast, with one last strike, smashed the altar. His gear body and pieces flew everywhere. The jewel lay on the floor as Clockwork Knight began to crawl to it. Its majestic yet calming force sent out a pulse wave that could be seen across the floor.

Samantha, frightened and crying, called out, "Clockwork Knight! Are you all right? Hang on! I'll call for a rescue team. My com link is dead. What do I do?"

Clockwork Knight spoke with difficulty, "Milady, my pr . . . inc . . . ess, do not be a . . . fraid; claim the je . . . wel and go whe . . . ere it calls thee. Our home Des . . . ern . . . a beckons. You . . . have . . . a destiny to ful . . . fill Please . . . mi . . . la . . . dy. I know . . . you . . . can do . . . it."

Samantha begged, "No, please!, I need you!" She began crying harder than before. She spoke around her sobs. "You helped me . . . when I had nobody. You can't leave me now! . . . I haven't . . . we haven't gone home yet. We were supposed to build a new Deserna here on this planet. Please don't go!" She poured all of her emotion out.

She held his wrecked body in her arms, and his eyes looked at her gently. She left him for a moment to claim the jewel and returned to his side. He looked at her one last time then his eyes turned gray. Samantha looked at the jewel then got up as the tears continued down her face. The forest stronghold began to implode as Samantha vanished.

★   ★   ★

The magnificent light pierced the dense foliage, and the old keeper of the Pagama lord's palace saw and smiled. The old man wondered to himself, "I wonder which one it is this time. He chuckled. Two of the three have been found. Will a true lord of the Pagama emerge from the trials?"

Samantha's log to be continued . . .

CHRONICLE LOG

AERO MARSH

HAGGLESBEE'S LOG BEGINS . . .

HAGGLESBEE WAS IN HIS SHIP FLYING THROUGH HEAVY STORM WINDS.

"HMMMM, MAYBE IT'S BECAUSE OF THE STRONG WINDS? THAT COULD BE CAUSING THE WATERS TO STAY FROZEN FOR SUCH A LONG TIME AND SO HARD THAT THE SUN CAN'T MELT IT. WELL, I'M HERE NOW, SO THERE'S NO TURNING BACK."

HIS GEAR BURNERS ACTIVATED.

HAGGLESBEE FLEW OFF INTO THE TURBULENT WINDSTORM AS THE METAL WAS BEING RIPPED TO SHREDS. THE HORRIFYING WINDS TORE THROUGH IT LIKE KNIVES PIERCING HOT BUTTER BUT HAGGLESBEE DIVED FOR AN EMERGENCY LANDING, FALLING BELOW THE DEVASTATING STORM CLOUDS. HE LANDED HARD, BREAKING THE LANDING GEAR ON THE AIRCRAFT; HE CHECKED HIS GEAR AND THEN EXITED THE FIGHTER. HE WALKED BUT A FEW STEPS BEFORE SOMETHING FLUNG HIM INTO THE AIR. VIOLENT WINDS THREW HIM INTO THE ROCKS; HAGGLESBEE GOT UP AND LOOKED AROUND, ONLY TO HEAR VOICES SAY, "WHO ARE YOU?"

"WIND WRAITHS! I'VE HEARD OF THESE; THEY'RE LOST SOULS WHO HAVE FLOWN THESE TERRIBLE SKIES ONLY TO BE CUT DOWN."

HE WAS AGAIN FLUNG INTO THE AIR. HE HIT THE GROUND AND ACTIVATED HIS GRAPPLE BRACELET AS HE WAS FLUNG INTO THE AIR ONCE MORE. USING HIS GOGGLES, HE LOCATED SOME RUINS AND GRAPPLED TO THEM TO ESCAPE THE WIND WRAITHS. LOOKING AROUND, HE ACTIVATED HIS LIGHT PENDANT, WHICH WAS LOCATED ON HIS BELT. IT ILLUMINATED HIS WAY THROUGH THE EERIE DARK PASSAGES. AS HAGGLESBEE WENT ON, HE WAS ASTOUNDED TO SEE THAT HE HAD ENTERED THE RESTING PLACE OF THE RUBY. A COLD BREEZE FROM THE UPPER PART OF THE RUINS EDGES CLOSER TO THE WIND-FILLED CORRIDORS.

"HMM, SHOULD I GO UP OR DOWN? MAYBE THESE ARE TRAPS OF SOME SORT?"

HAGGLESBEE CONTINUED LOOKING AT THE ANCIENT SIGNS USING HIS MAPPER'S DECODER TO DECIPHER THEIR MEANINGS. IF ANYTHING, HE WAS TRYING TO SOLVE THEIR MIND-BOGGLING CLUES. HE SAT FOR A WHILE TO CATCH HIS BREATH AND REST HIS FEET. HE POPPED OPEN HIS CANTEEN AND DRANK A FEW SIPS OF WATER. AFTERWARD, HAGGLESBEE GOT UP AND STARTED LOOKING AROUND. HE NOTICED HE COULD NOT HEAR THE WIND ON THE OUTSIDE. HE WALKED FARTHER ALONG AND THEN HEARD FOOTSTEPS. FIRST, THE FOOTSTEPS SEEMED TO BE IN FRONT OF HIM, BUT THEN HE HEARD THE STEPS BEHIND HIM. KNOWING HE HEARD SOMEONE BEHIND HIM, HAGGLESBEE BACKTRACKED, BUT THERE WAS NO LONGER ANY SOUND. HE DECIDED TO USE SOME STRING HE HAD IN HIS PACK. STARTING FROM THE BEGINNING OF THE ROUTE TO THE TEMPLE, HE USED DAGGERS AND STRING STUCK INTO THE GROUND. THE FIRST PATH HE WALKED AGAIN; HEARING NO WIND, HE WENT AS FAR AS HE COULD, NOT STOPPING UNTIL HE REACHED A DEAD END. HE RETURNED TO THE BEGINNING AGAIN. AS HE DID, HE NOTICED THAT THE ENTRANCE THAT HAD BEEN UNSEALED WAS NOW SEALED WITH NO POSSIBLE EXIT. THE ONLY CHOICE WAS TO GO FORWARD, THIS TIME USING THE SECOND PATH. HAGGLESBEE WENT DOWN THE PATH AGAIN, AND AS BEFORE, HE HEARD FOOTSTEPS. HE QUICKLY TURNED AROUND BUT SAW NOTHING THERE. HE CONTINUED ON, FIRST GOING STRAIGHT AND THEN TURNING LEFT AND LEFT AGAIN; HE NEXT WENT RIGHT UNTIL AGAIN HE WAS AT A DEAD END. HAGGLESBEE TURNED AROUND, BUT THIS TIME, SOMETHING

WAS TUGGING ON HIS STRING. HE HURRIED BACK AND SAW A SHADOWY FIGURE MOVE FARTHER AWAY AND DOWN THE CORRIDOR.

"WAIT!" HE SHOUTED. "ARE YOU FRIEND OR FOE? ARE YOU ANOTHER MAPPER?"

THERE WAS NO ANSWER, SO HE RETURNED TO THE ENTRANCE, WITH NOTHING CHANGED. HAGGLESBEE COULDN'T UNDERSTAND WHY THERE HAD BEEN A TUG ON THE STRING. WHAT WAS THE MYSTERIOUS SHADOW? HE STOPPED WALKING AROUND AND WONDERED FOR A MOMENT TO HIMSELF. HE THEN CONTINUED ON TO THE THIRD CORRIDOR BUT DIDN'T NOTICE THE TINY HOLES IN THE WALL. AS HE MOVED DOWN THE PASSAGE, A SMALL NEEDLE SHOT OUT AT HIM. HE DUCKED JUST IN TIME. IT BARELY MISSED HIM. HE CAME OUT OF IT WITH ONLY A FEW MINOR SCRAPES AND BRUISES. WHEN HE GOT TO THE END, IT HAD LOOPED AROUND INTO THE FOURTH CORRIDOR LIKE A GIANT HORSESHOE. HAGGLESBEE LAUGHED AT HIMSELF AS HE CAME AROUND BACK TO THE START AND SAW HIS STRINGS. FROM THE SMALL HOLES IN THE RUINS, HE COULD TELL IT WAS BECOMING NIGHT.

"SEVEN HOURS," HE SAID. "SEVEN HOURS WASTED. MAYBE NOT . . . MAYBE IT WAS SEVEN HOURS TO LEARN."

WHAT HAGGLESBEE LEARNED WAS THAT THE POSITION OF THE SUN AND WIND MOVED THE CORRIDORS AROUND, THEREBY FOOLING TRAVELERS INTO THINKING THERE WAS NO EXIT OR WAY AROUND. HAGGLESBEE SAT AWHILE ANALYZING THE PROBLEM, AS HE DID HE FINALLY REACHED A CONCLUSION. HE FIGURED OUT THAT IT WAS NOT A SHADOW OF SOMEONE ELSE HE HAD SEEN BUT A SHADOW OF WHERE THE ROOMS CHANGED AND THE FOOTSTEPS HE HAD HEARD HAD TO BE FROM A DEVICE OF SOME SORT. HE CHECKED ALL HIS CONCLUSIONS, GOING TO THE EXACT PLACES THEY HAPPENED. EVEN THOUGH IT WAS NOW NIGHT, THE SAME THING HAPPENED AGAIN AS HAGGLESBEE THOUGHT IT WOULD. THE ROOMS CHANGED, REVEALING A ROCK FORMATION THAT LOOKED LIKE A PERSON AND A SMALL MIRROR TO REFLECT THE LIGHT SO IF SOMEONE WAS IN THERE, HE OR SHE WOULD BE FRIGHTENED AND LOSE HIS OR HER SENSE OF DIRECTION, CREATING CONFUSION. THE

FOOTSTEPS WERE CREATED BY A PRIMITIVE NUTSHELL MECHANISM THAT SIMULATED FOOTSTEPS. AFTER FIGURING OUT THE RUINS' TRICKERY, HAGGLESBEE WAS ABLE TO MOVE FARTHER ALONG INSIDE THE WIND LABYRINTH. HE OPENED THE FIFTH PASSAGEWAY, AND THE REAL GAME BEGAN AS HUGE STONE DOORS CLOSED TIGHT BEHIND HIM.

SOON, POISONOUS FUMES ENTERED THE ROOM. HAGGLESBEE LOOKED AROUND CALMLY AND SAW A TYPE OF MURAL PUZZLE. THE POISONOUS FUMES CREPT CLOSER, INCHING UPWARD. THE FLOOR BEGAN TO BREAK AWAY; BELOW IT WAS A PIT FILLED WITH THE POISONOUS FUMES. HAGGLESBEE CONTINUED, NOT LOOKING BACK AS HE MOVED PIECE AFTER PIECE, SOMETIMES RIGHT SOMETIMES WRONG. AT LAST, IT WAS ALMOST FINISHED.

ALL OF A SUDDEN, THE GIMMEES APPEARED. HIS MONSTER CODER WENT OFF, SHOWING HIM THEIR INFORMATION. THESE SMALL CREATURES STARTED TO TAKE APART THE PUZZLE. HAGGLESBEE GOT ANGRY BUT HAD NO TIME TO LOSE OR DEATH WOULD CLAIM HIM. THINKING QUICKLY, HE REDID THE PUZZLE JUST LIKE BEFORE, BUT THIS TIME, HE NOTICED THAT WHEN THE SUN HIT A CERTAIN SPOT, IT REFLECTED A GLARE. THE GIMMEES STOPPED AS IF THEY WERE MESMERIZED BY THE SHINE. HE TOOK OUT HIS GLASSES AND SET THEM DOWN IN THE SUN'S PATH. THE GIMMEES WERE INSTANTLY ATTRACTED TO THEM AND ALLOWED HIM TO FINISH THE PUZZLE THEN ESCAPE THE ROOM. HOWEVER, THE POISONOUS FUMES WERE IN THE NEXT ROOM; THIS TIME, THE FLOOR HAD SPIKES STICKING UP AND DOWN. HAGGLESBEE COULDN'T TELL WHEN THE NEXT ONE WOULD COME BECAUSE OF THE FUME CLOUD ACROSS THE FLOOR. HE FIGURED OUT THE MURAL PUZZLE, WITH THE GIMMEES DOING THEIR JOB. BUT THE MURAL DEPICTED A RUIN HUNTER AND THEM AIDING ONE ANOTHER IN THE WIND LABYRINTH.

NOW, WITH THE DOOR CLOSED BEHIND HIM, HE BEGAN THINKING TO HIMSELF, HOW DO I GET THE GLASSES BACK AND HELP THEM? WAIT A MINUTE; I KNOW!

HE LOOKED THROUGH HIS POCKETS AND FOUND A LIGHT PEN. HE SAW AN OPENING IN THE WALL TO THE LAST ROOM AND FLASHED THE PEN. THEY CAME TO IT IMMEDIATELY ONCE MORE. THEY AIDED

EACH OTHER THROUGH THE WATER TRAP, THE FIRE BARRAGE, AND THE WIND SPIRES. THE WATER TRAP WAS A ROOM FILLED WITH WATER. HAGGLESBEE HAD TO LURE THE GIMMEES INTO A WATER WHEEL SO THAT THEY COULD TURN IT. HE CLEVERLY BEGAN TO RUN IN A CIRCULAR MOTION UNTIL THEY MOVED THE WHEEL. THEY ALL SURVIVED AND MOVED ON. THE FIRE BARRAGE TRAPS WERE HUGE WIND-POWERED AIR GUNS THAT RAINED DOWN GIANT BALLS OF FLAME. HAGGLESBEE COULD NOT DODGE ALL OF THE EXPLOSIONS. HE SAW THAT IT WAS LIKE A DANCE, MOVING AROUND THE FLAMES WITHOUT BEING HIT. HE HAD TO POSITION THE GIMMEES IN FORMATION SO THAT AT A CERTAIN TIME, THE AIR GUN WOULD STOP WHEN THE FLOOR LEVER WAS PRESSED. THE STEPS WERE LIKE A DANCE THAT CAME TOGETHER PERFECTLY. THEY MADE IT PAST THE FIRE. LAST WERE THE WIND SPIRES, FOR THIS TRAP, HE WAS IN ONE ROOM AND THE GIMMEES IN ANOTHER.

"HMMM, HOW CAN I ACT WITH THEM WITHOUT BEING IN CLOSE CONTACT?" HE WONDERED.

THAT WAS WHEN HE DISCOVERED THE WIND LAUNCHER. HE HAD TO BLOW A CERTAIN HORN AT THE RIGHT TIME TO LAUNCH EACH GIMMEE AT A HUGE ANCHOR IN THE MIDDLE OF THE ROOM. TWO WALLS OF WIND BLOCKED HIS PATH, HE SHOT THEM AT THE ANCHOR AND THEY FORMED A CHAIN. THEY PULLED THE CEILING DOWN, CAUSING THE HUGE WALL OF WIND AS WELL AS THE ENTRANCE TO BE COVERED BY ROCK. HAGGLESBEE THOUGHT UP ANOTHER SOLUTION, THIS TIME REROUTING THE AIR INTO A PRESSURIZED WIND CANNON WITH HELP FROM THE GIMMEES, HE CREATED A WIND DUCT USING THE HEAVY WOODEN STRUCTURES FROM THE WRECKAGE. NEXT, HE TOOK OUT A STICK OF DYNAMITE BUT REALIZED THE WIND GUSTS WOULD ONLY PUT OUT THE FLAME. SO HE DECIDED TO SHOOT A ROCK THROUGH IT TO CRACK THE OTHER ROCK IN TWO. IT WORKED. HE SMASHED THE OTHER ROCK BUT ONLY THE TOP PART. HE COULD SEE THE DOOR SMASHED OPEN ON THE TOP A BIT SO HE CRAWLED THROUGH ONLY TO SEE AN EVEN BIGGER DOOR.

"THE GIMMEES ARE GONE, EH? NO MORE TRICKS, SO IT WOULD SEEM. WHATEVER'S IN THERE IS IN THERE."

HE ENTERED THE ROOM TO SEE A JEWEL ON ONE SIDE. THE DOOR CLOSED BEHIND HIM. HE LOOKED AROUND CAUTIOUSLY. SOON, THE FLOOR BEGAN TO RISE. ENORMOUS ANCIENT STONE PILLARS PAVED A PATH TO THE JEWEL THAT LAY ON THE OTHER SIDE. AS HAGGLESBEE WALKED ACROSS, HE COULD FEEL A STRONG GUST OF AIR. JUST AS HE WAS ABOUT TO TOUCH THE GEM, A HUGE CREATURE APPEARED SO SWIFTLY HE WAS CAUGHT OFF GUARD.

"SO, YET ANOTHER APPEARS BEFORE ME, EH? FOOLISH LITTLE BEING, YE LET TREASURE CLOUD YOUR MIND."

HAGGLESBEE COULD FEEL THE CREATURE'S BREATH ON HIS SHOULDER. IT WAS CLOSER THAN HE THOUGHT.

"THIS JEWEL IS ONE OF THE FIVE SACRED STONES NEEDED TO ENTER THE KING'S ROAD. I HAVE BRAVED THIS LABYRINTH AND BESTED ITS TRIALS."

"I AM THE GUARDIAN BEAST, AERO FANG. YET AGAIN, ANOTHER FOOLISH TRAVELER COMES TO ME ONLY FOR MY FANGS TO BE COLORED CRIMSON."

"I AM A PEACEFUL MAN," SAID HAGGLESBEE. "I'M A SEEKER OF KNOWLEDGE, AN ADVENTURER."

AND THUS, HAGGLESBEE ENGAGED IN BATTLE WITH THE TITANIC BEAST. HE CHARGED UP HIS ENERGY AND BLASTED AT AERO FANG. AERO FANG DODGED WITH PRECISE ACCURACY, WALKING ALONGSIDE THE BLAST, AND THEN POUNCED. HAGGLESBEE RAN IN FEAR AND TERROR. HE CALMED HIMSELF EVEN THOUGH HE STILL TREMBLED THEN BEGAN TO NOTICE THAT THE AREA HAD AIR HOLES WHERE THE PATH TO THE JEWEL LED, BUT IT WAS GONE. HE SAW THAT IF ONE TIMED ONE'S JUMPS, ONE COULD AIR-BLAST UP TO THE JEWEL ALTAR. AERO FANG ROARED WITH A HUGE BLAST OF WIND EXPLODING FROM ITS MOUTH. HAGGLESBEE DODGED, TRIPPING OVER HIS OWN FEET AND THEN ROLLED OVER THE LEDGE CLOSEST TO HIM. AS HE FELL, HE GRABBED ONTO A RAILING WITH HIS FALSE HAND WHILE DANGLING ON THE SIDE THEN PULLED HIMSELF UP BY CATCHING A WIND

DRAFT. HE LANDED NEAR THE ALTAR, BUT AERO FANG APPEARED IN FRONT OF HIM AND ALMOST TOOK HIS HEAD OFF. HAGGLESBEE USED ALL OF HIS ENERGY IN ONE HUGE BLAST, KNOCKING THE BEAST TO THE GROUND. WHILE THE BEAST WAS DOWN, HE TOOK A JET STREAM MAKING IT TO THE JEWEL ALTAR. AS HE TOUCHED IT, HE BEGAN TO FLY.

AERO FANG LAUGHED QUIETLY. "IT WAS ALL ABOUT KNOWLEDGE HERE, NOT FIGHTING ME. I AM A BEAST OF KNOWLEDGE. AYE, PRAY THEE A KIND AND BENEVOLENT KING ASCENDS THE THRONE."

THE TEMPLE AREA CALLED THE AERO MARSH SOON TURNED TO WIND AND VANISHED. HAGGLESBEE FLEW THROUGH THE SKY AND VANISHED AS WELL.

HAGGLESBEE LOG TO BE CONTINUED . . .

CHRONICLE LOG

Magma Glaciers

Jex asked, "Is it true? Are we going home?"

"Really? We can go back to our home world?" asked Annie.

G said, "Yep, folks; we're going home back to our Pagama. Unfortunately though, it's not OUR Pagama anymore."

Oil said, "Yeah, they said this planet popped up all of a sudden."

"And let me guess," said G. "It's a giant real estate profit, right?"

Oil said, "Yeah. They said Neo Pagama is a utopian paradise ready and willing for the making."

"You think so?" said Jex. "It would appear to me that if a Pagama leader came forward, the other planets or universal leaders would try to control them since it's a planet rebuilding itself."

"Oh boy!" G said, rubbing his head. "Planet politics. Good grief."

Annie, shocked, said, "G, we're getting a transmission. It's a job."

Hmm, that was fast, thought G. "Anyhoo, what's the job, Annie?"

Annie's eyes were bugging out in awe. "G . . . G . . . G, look at this!"

G got up and looked at the screen. He fell back into his seat and rubbed his head.

"Woo-hoo!" shouted an excited Jex.

"G, we're rich," said Oil.

"Five million up front, and . . ." said G.

"*And*?" the others asked with gleeful faces.

"Seventy-five million upon completion and full deliverance of the item that we're supposed to recover," G explained.

"Eighty million?" said Jex. "What's this job we have that's so important?"

"Where would anyone get that much bread?" asked Annie.

"So what's the job?" asked Oil.

"We're headed down to planet Neo Pagama to some place called the Magma Glaciers," said G. "From there, we're supposed to investigate the place, find some treasure, and the rest is history, folks. Take us down, Jex. The coordinates are already downloaded into our navigation systems."

The ship thrusters ignited, and they headed for their destination. It was a smooth descent into Neo Pagama. The ship, the *Rusty Angel*, landed at the Magma Glaciers, a place both deadly and beautiful. Magma erupted from the planet's rage as the crew opened the bomb-bay doors. Oil prepared the gear. Annie set up their com and navi units (navigator units).

"Jex, careful of those magma spires," warned G. "That stuff is thirty thousand degrees. It's hotter than normal."

"Whatever, man; I can handle it," said Jex, checking the landing cameras.

"I want to get home in one piece to enjoy my money, Jex," Annie said and smiled.

"Yeah," said Oil.

"Shuddup," Jex said and laughed. Watch yer backs; I hear there are shine officer ships all over the place.

"Cool it," said G. "Get focused."

The ship landed at a clearing, but the area was unstable.

"This geography is weird, G. The land is chaotic and unstable. There wasn't any other place to land," said Annie.

"G," said Oil, "I'm in the vehicle bay. The tank is set up. We're ready to go."

Jex said, "Come back, okay? Or she's mine."

"The *Rusty Angel*, she won't stand for another captain, you know!, never!," said G. They smacked hands.

"I don't know how long this field is going to hold," said Jex. "We should really upgrade our force-field system."

"Sure," G said, looking up. "As soon as we pick up that eighty million. Oil, let's roll out."

The vehicle-bay doors opened on the unstable terrain. The land-terrain vehicle, the drag breaker, blasted out full speed, headed into the magma hardened terrain and intense heat.

"Woo, man!" said Oil, wiping his forehead. "It's crazy hot, G."

"Yeah, it is! But stay cool; the AC's blasting," said G. "Did you just see that?"

"What?" asked Oil. "There's nothing on the sensors or the scanners. Wait! I just saw a blip really quick. What . . . ?"

The drag breaker moved across the smoldering land. From the clouded black sky, a fireball collided with the tank. G stopped jerking the wheel which caused the vehicle to tailspin and stop short before they fell into a lava pit."

"What the heck was that?" asked G.

"It was a fireball; that thing was huge!" said Oil.

"Fireballs don't just collide with people, now do they?" asked G, smirking.

From the flames, a huge pyro cat appeared. It walked slowly as the ground burned. Oil and G were still groggy but soon find their enemy was before them.

"Oil, get in the back! Hurry!" shouted G.

Oil moved into the back compartment as the doors opened to reveal a gun-blaster turret. Oil fired off ice shells. One was not enough to stop the pyro cat, which had begun its assault. Oil fired more shots off, freezing the beast. Meanwhile, another pyro cat appeared in front of them. G hit the pedal, and the tank took off, hitting the pyro cat as the others began their pursuit.

"Wow! These things can move!" said Oil.

"Stop admiring their speed and keep shooting!" ordered G.

G maneuvered the drag breaker through the rough terrain and magma fissures. The ground began to erupt with lava spewing forth with rock exploding everywhere. G was doing his best as the ground began to crumble. The drag breaker was about to fall, but G hit a button that activated the cannon drive boosters. These boosters drew in energy from around the heated air, providing them with explosive power as they were lifted to safety.

G was sweating. "Man, that was an eye-opener."

"Can't you drive?" said Oil, breathing frantically.

G laughed. "All part of being a crew member of the *Rusty Nails*."

"I should have become a salesman like my family wanted. Noooooo, I had to join G-force jets crew." Head hanging, Oil muttered, "Why me? Why me?"

They moved on; the pyro cats were long gone. But soon, the rock began erupting once more. It looked like it was smooth sailing . . .

"Oil, ahhhh. Hang on, Oil. Where are you?" asked G.

By the time Oil looked, he was in the air. G was strapped in and could do nothing about it. G watched as Oil flew, but the tank was flying, not Oil. The tank tumbled over and over again, but at the same time, the cannon blaster in the back fell and was ripped to pieces. It then exploded, propelling the tank, causing even more damage. By the time the tank landed, it was too badly damaged. G was bleeding heavily and trying to figure out what had happened. G saw that Oil was on the ground, and the flames were erupting from the ground. From inside of the treacherous flame, a huge beast made of magma and iron emerged. These were called magma growls. They were Titanic creatures more terrifying than pyro cats; one moved slowly toward Oil as he opened his eyes, reaching and feeling around for his glasses. G screamed, but his efforts were in vain. The magma growl moved slowly then suddenly picked up speed. G fumbled with the controls, trying to ignite the tank. He managed to hit the fuel pedal as the tank sped toward Oil and the magma growl. G screamed, "Get out of the way!"

Oil saw G and rolled out of the way. G jumped out of the tank as the magma growl went after Oil. The tank hit the beast and exploded on impact. A powerful explosive force caused further eruptions to occur on the already unstable terrain.

"Oil!" G called his name multiple times. "You okay? Come on! Wake up! We got to go!"

"Uh, where am I?" said Oil in a tired voice.

Before they could catch their breath, more pyro cats appeared. They were surrounded. G was out of options and did not know what to do next.

Annie's voice could be heard through static. "G, there's a hole. Temple . . . Where . . . You . . . are . . . jump."

"Hole? What hole?" asked G. "I can't hear you, Annie."

Running, Oil yelled, "Move!"

G used his det pack (detonator pack), and they escaped down a hole. The pyro cats pounced and exploded on contact with each other as G and Oil fall a long distance. When they came to, G couldn't move his arm feeling that his arm was broken and his teeth were loose while Oil discovered his leg was broken. The two adventurers were exhausted from the heated area as they watched lava erupting and pour forth.

"Whoever sent us on this run is going to pay for this, 'cause nobody messes with me or my crew. Nobody! You hear me. All right, Oil, according to this navi watch, we got enemies on the right, left, up, and down, so basically, we're surrounded," said G.

"Sorry I couldn't be stronger, G," replied Oil.

"That's okay," said G. "I'll be stronger for the both of us. Being strong doesn't necessarily make you a man; it's a combination of things, like cooking, and cooking's like alchemy."

"Right, G," said Oil, rebandaging his leg, "so we could split up or keep moving since all the intel is in the navi watch. We got the monsters or whatever's in here with us and treasure locations."

"Well, we're not exploring nothing; we're bee lining it straight to whatever is here and getting the heck outta here!" said G.

*   *   *

Meanwhile, on board the Rusty Angel . . .

"Darn this magma," said Jex. "Not to mention this heat. You would think in the year twenty-five eighty-two we would have technological advancements that can get around this natural interference."

"Hey," Annie said, "it's nature. What do you expect?"

"We've advanced so far," said Jex. "I want to see. To surpass these mysterious runes' magic and energies; that's why I joined G's crew, the Rusty Nails. I seek more."

"Why not just join the Shine Institute of Technology? they're always studying that stuff or you could find those mystical relic hunters, the Mappers. Now, enough of this, let's get back to trying to locate G and Oil." replied Annie.

*   *   *

Oil and G were on the move. Suddenly, fire creatures burst forth from the walls. These were pyrosaurs, the flame Lizardians. G's eyes were open wide with fear; he couldn't believe it.

"Hokey smokes! Lizardians and they're on fire. Oil, run! Hurry!"

"G, what about you? I can't make it alone. You have to come with me!" Oil was breathing hard and sweating.

"Here, take the navi watch," said G. He threw the watch to Oil.

Oil took off running as well as he could with his hurt leg. G turned around and saw nothing but flames.

"So, it has come to this," said G. "I didn't want to use this." He looked down at his wrist. "Well, let's rock and roll. Scale bags, I need a new suit and shoes." He activated the elemental geo. "T.I.P activate," he said, referring to thermo ignition power, which allowed a geo user to draw power from the sun. Since the heat was so intense in the temple, G could draw power from it to use.

"I feel it all right! HEY You!" A powerful flame aura rose around him. "Scale bags, time to get smoked!"

G used the top-secret power bracelet called elemental geo, soaking up the power of the flames around him. G threw out his fist, blasting them with a more powerful flame, which extinguished the pyrosaurs. More appeared from the flames as his visor detected them on his right and center, leaving the left open to move. G flipped in the air then clapped his hands together, creating a shock wave of flame, which put theirs out, making them begin to evaporate quickly. More Pyrosaurs arrived from the flames as he continued to do battle with them, not backing down. He leg-swept the floor, sending out a flame wave, which tripped them. G came down after jumping high using his rocket boosters powered by the flames. A huge down pour of flames covered the floor, extinguishing all the flames in that part of the room.

After the fight, G's scan visor began to tell him that ahead was a huge heat source, along with a maze like corridor. The scan visor also gave him more information about the heat around his body. Soon, G took off and flew by using the flames near his feet.

Meanwhile . . .

Oil made it to the altar room; soon, the flames began to grow more intense. As he got closer, his clothes began to burn. Oil activated his burn suit, but he could still feel the heat and continued sweating.

"Amazing," said Oil. "I never imagined this was the power of the prototype." He was breathing heavily. "Got to get to the end."

From afar, Oil could see a jewel of some sort. He tried to get closer, but the flames grew more intense.

"Yes," said Oil, "I can see it. What the . . . ?" He screamed.

Oil was thrown across the room as a tribeast appeared from the mighty flames.

It had three flaming heads and was ready for full battle—not a mark on its body. Oil suspected he was the first to arrive there. Oil saw nothing but a beast of pure fire. The beast warrior's eyes stayed on Oil as he trembled. The fire beast Gourin moved slowly; as flames exploded from its feet, causing the area to spike in a heat burst. Oil was petrified to his soul as his mind goes blank. G arrived looking at Gourin and the altar of flames. His visor was telling him his flame output was reaching danger levels. The tribeast Gourin's other heads appeared from the flames on its body. They gazed at G. Not wasting any time, he rushed in to fight. As he ran, the visor told him his power levels were at maximum capacity. Gourin's mouth opened, and a barrage of mammoth flames poured out toward G. It wasn't a regular flame attack; it sounded like a flamethrower. The scanner picked up the reading, telling him it was white fire, the hottest flame in existence. G punched both of his hands forward causing a huge blast. Gourin fired at the same time. The flames collided in a power struggle; G held his ground at first but slowly began slipping. He rolled out of the way as Oil moved toward the altar thinking he could end the battle quickly. As Oil climbed, his hands began to burn almost to the bone, he fell screaming in pain. G flew to the altar and almost grasped the jewel, but Gourin appeared from the white-hot flames in a fantastic ball of white fire. His mighty paw of pure flame smacked G away, causing him to hit fiery pillar after fiery pillar. G got up angrier than before and without thinking, he flew at Gourin in full rage, kicking the air, which caused a flame burst that hit the mighty Beast Gourin, knocking it down. G held out his arm, and a flamethrower blast exploded from his hand. He pushed Gourin back, knocking out one of its flaming heads. The other two looked around, searching for G. They couldn't find him. Suddenly, G came crashing down from the air in a pillar of flames, hitting Gourin. The area exploded in a barrage of fire and explosions. While that was happening, Oil crawled closer to the altar as G got up with Gourin temporarily defeated, he hovered over to Oil. He saw his friend was struggling to breathe.

"Here, Oil," he said. "Breathe in slowly. Come on; you can do it. That's it. Sit tight; I'll be right back."

He then turned toward the altar of flames. Reaching into them, he soon felt a powerful wave of energy. The elemental geo went crazy sending information all over the visor screen.

"The power of flame, a power of the gods wielded by a man, a power that no other can ever comprehend, combine all fire, water, earth, wind and light. Combine them all to gain the power that is forbidden. The power of Olmgala, a power that has not been seen since the beginning. What's this . . . Empire of the Dragon . . . Emperor of All Flame . . ."

G's visor opened, and he looked at Oil.

The temple began to break down as the magma and white flames exploded around them. G grabbed Oil, and a powerful blast exploded from his feet propelling him like a flamethrower, flying them up, dodging the rocks and flaming debris that fell trying to bury them. He soon saw an opening.

"Oil," said G, "it seems the flames bother you." He was staring at the ruby of fire like he was mesmerized.

"Yeah, but not you," said Oil. "Where'd you get that gear? G? . . . G! Hey, buddy, you okay?"

"Well, if you can't stand the heat." G hit Oil with a full two-fist flamethrower, burning him to nothingness.

He left as the temple fell. A huge pillar of energy exploded toward the sky. The Old Caretaker saw this and was saddened.

*   *   *

Back at the Magma Glaciers . . .
G made it back to the *Rusty Angel.*

"Annie, get to the bridge; we got to get outta here. G's back," said Jex.

He walked to the crew area.

"G, where's Oil?" asked Jex.

"We have to get out of here. Things are heating up." G said in a calm tone

"I've been doing some research. Is that the fabled Loom Ruby? It exists. I also heard this on the com. Listen." asked Jex

The tape began to play.
"It appears you can't stand the heat."

"Yeah," said Oil's voice.

The tape ended.

"Why, G?" asked Jex. "Why, Captain?"

Suddenly, the tribeast Gourin appeared once more. This time, its body was orange flame colored and not white fire any longer.

"Well now," said G, "it appears the beast will not bow to me."

"What? Where did that thing come from?" asked Jex. "Annie, let's go blast off."

"I'm no longer G. I am the emperor of flame, leader of the Dragon Empire. I am Igneous. If you wish death, so be it."

"G, stop!" yelled Jex, taking out his stun rifle.

The entire ship and the surrounding area exploded into a massive vortex of white flames. G/Igneous stood among the flames as they surrounded his body.

"The throne of the king beckons me on to greater things," declared G/Igneous.

G/Igneous took off as the magma glaciers erupted and the lava spewed forth.

G's log end . . .

*   *   *

Through the light snowfall, figures moved about. Why, dear friends, it is our old adventurers Corsx and Burn!

What are they up to, hmm?

CHRONICLE LOG

ICE CITADEL

CONTINUED

CORSX LOG RESTART . . .

"SO, YOU BOYS GOING BACK INTO THE ICE CITADEL, EH? GETTING YOUR TAILS HANDED TO YOU THE FIRST TIME WASN'T ENOUGH, HUH?" MOASSA SAID AND LAUGHED. SHE WAS EATING BREAKFAST.

"EH," SAID BURN, SHRUGGING HIS SHOULDERS, "IF AT FIRST YOU DON'T SUCCEED . . ."

"GET BEAT UP SOME MORE," SAID CORSX.

GINA SAID, "THE CHOPPER'S READY FOR FLIGHT. THE GEAR IS READY TOO."

"YEAH," SAID ZORBOR. "GOOD LUCK, GUYS. MY CREW DIDN'T MAKE IT BACK. BUT YOU WILL."

"THE NEW BOOSTERS ARE READY AND HOTTER THAN EVER," SAID BURN. "YOU READY, BUD?"

"WELL, NOW THAT WE'RE READY, MOVE OUT," ORDERED CORSX.

"HEY, CORSX, OLD BUD, YOU AREN'T RIDING WITH ME?" ASKED BURN.

"I GOT MY MOTO-WAKI WORKING. IT WAS JUST DELIVERED, SO I'LL USE THAT."

"YOU GUYS COME BACK SAFELY," SAID ZORBOR.

MOASSA SAID, "AFTER YOU GUYS MOVE OUT, I'LL BE RIGHT BEHIND YOU IN THE TRUCK."

"AYE, AYE, LET'S MOVE OUT," THEY ALL SAID IN UNISON.

"GEARED TO GO! I LOVE SAYING THAT," SAID BURN, GRINNING.

"GEARED TO GO!" SAID CORSX, GIVING THE THUMBS-UP SIGNAL.

THEY MOVED OUT. GINA WAS HAVING AN EASY TIME UNTIL SHE REACHED THE WINDS AROUND THE ICE CITADEL.

THEN ALL OF A SUDDEN . . .

GINA YELLED, "GUYS, COME IN . . ." HER VOICE FADED IN AND OUT WITH STATIC. "OH NO!" SHE SCREAMED.

"SO YOU DARE COME BACK, EH?" SAID A VOICE. "ONLY THOSE TWO ARE NEEDED. GREAT POWERS OF DARKNESS, HEED MY CALL. FROM THE BLACKEST PITCH, RELEASE YOUR EVIL SCOURGED PAIN."

A HUGE BLACK BOLT FELL FROM THE BLIZZARD-FILLED SKY. IT HIT THE TAIL BLADE OF HER CRAFT CAUSING HER TO SPIN OUT OF CONTROL. SHE WAS NOT ABLE TO EJECT IN TIME. IT WAS IF SOMETHING HAD A HOLD ON THE WINDOW. AS SHE LOOKED, SHE SAW AGONIZED AND TORMENTED SOULS HANGING ON TO THE WINDOW. SHE SCREAMED IN HORROR AS THE HELICOPTER HIT THE GROUND AND BURST INTO FLAMES.

*   *   *

BURN AND CORSX FOUND THE WRECKAGE.

"NOTHING WE CAN DO," SAID BURN. HE PUSHED THE WRECKAGE ASIDE, USING HIS BULLDOZER SHIELD.

THEY CONTINUED ON DEEPER INTO THE TREACHEROUS AND FRIGID GRIP OF THE BLIZZARD. HAVING MADE IT TO THE ICE CITADEL ONCE MORE, THEY NOTICED THAT THERE WAS A DOOR WHERE THERE HADN'T BEEN ONE BEFORE. BURN BUSTED THE DOOR DOWN, AND CORSX FOLLOWED. THEY SLOWLY MOVED THROUGH THE HALLS OF THE TEMPLE.

"HEY, CORSX," SAID BURN, "THE MAP WE MADE IS DIFFERENT."

"YEAH," SAID CORSX, "HOW COULD THIS PLACE CHANGE SO MUCH IN SUCH A SHORT TIME? BUT THAT'S IMPOSSIBLE."

FROM UNDERNEATH THEM, A HUGE ICE GATOR ROSE UP AND USED ITS MASSIVE JAWS TO RIP CORSX'S MOTO-WAKI TO SHREDS AS

IT DRAGGED IT TO THE COLD, MURKY DEPTHS. CORSX WAS ON THE ICE FLOOR.

BREATHING HARD, CORSX SAID, "AN ICE GATOR THAT WASN'T HERE BEFORE?"

"WE BETTER GET OUT OF HERE NOW," SAID BURN. "LET'S DO IT TO IT. HOP ON, CORSX. LET'S KICK SOME TAIL, LIKE IN THE OLD DAYS."

"YEAH," SAID CORSX.

"THIS TIME, I'LL TURN ON THE HEAT BACK THERE!" BURN LAUGHED.

*   *   *

"SO, ZORBOR, AFTER THIS, I GUESS WE BEGIN TO CLEAN UP AND START BUILDING," SAID MOASSA. SHE TURNED AROUND.

ZORBOR USED THE STUN LASER, AND SHE FELL UNCONSCIOUS.

"THE MASTER WILL BE PLEASED," HE SAID AND BEGAN LAUGHING INSANELY. "HIS WILL IS LAW AND SHALL SOON COME TO PASS."

HE LOCKED HER UP IN THE HOLDING AREA THEN STOLE THE RECON TRUCK VANISHING DEEPER INTO THE BLIZZARD, GETTING OUT IN A HURRY.

*   *   *

BACK AT THE CITADEL . . .

"GOOD GRIEF, MAN," SAID BURN.

CORSX SAID, "YIKES."

BURN AND CORSX WERE DUCKING AND DODGING ICEZARDIANS, WHICH APPEARED WITH INCREASING FREQUENCY.

"WE GOT TO SHAKE THEM AND KEEP MOVING; IT'S THE ONLY WAY," SAID BURN.

"KEEP DRIVING," SAID CORSX. "I'LL FIGURE SOMETHING OUT."

THEY MANAGED TO OUTRUN THE ICEZARDIANS, BUT SOON, THEY CAME TO AN UNDERGROUND ICE LAKE. BURN SPED IN FULL THROTTLE BUT THE ICE BEGAN CRACKING OPEN, REVEALING ICE HYDRAS FROM THE COLD DEPTHS. THEIR JAWS OPENED SHOOTING ICE BEAMS. BURN WAS DODGING THEM THE BEST HE COULD, BUT EVEN WITH ALL THE TRACTION HE HAD, IT WAS STILL TOO SLIPPERY. THEY MADE IT TO A WALL WITH THE HYDRAS IN PURSUIT. THINKING QUICKLY, HE USED THE ROCKET GRAPPLERS PULLING HIMSELF AND CORSX TO SAFETY.

"AN ICE LAKE," SAID CORSX. "WE NEVER SAW THAT BEFORE. MY LEGS, BURN, THEY ARE FREEZING." HIS TEETH WERE CHATTERING.

BURN ACTIVATED THE AUXILIARY HEATERS, MELTING THE ICE AROUND THE VEHICLE AND CORSX'S LEGS. CORSX SAT DOWN ON THE SIDE OF THE SNOW VEHICLE.

"BURN, I'VE MANAGED TO OVERLAY OUR OLD MAP WITH THIS NEW ONE. WE'RE WAY OFF COURSE," SAID CORSX.

"HMM. DO YOU SUPPOSE WE GOT LUCKY BEFORE SOMEHOW AND ENDED UP MISSING ALL THESE MONSTERS?" ASKED BURN.

"WAIT, BURN. THERE IT IS. THE SAME ROOM WE STOPPED AT. BUT IT'S TOO FAR AWAY FROM US."

"NO PROB," SAID BURN. "WE'LL USE THE GEAR BOOSTER'S MACH SEVEN. IF WE CAN'T GET BACK ON COURSE, WE'LL JUST MAKE OUR OWN, BUD."

"ARE YOU NUTS?" CORSX SAID. "I'M BACK HERE. THAT'S A LOAD OF GRAVITY FORCE TO HANDLE."

"DON'T WORRY, CORSX BROTHER," HE SAID AND GRINNED.

"WHEN YOU SAY 'BROTHER,' THAT USUALLY MEANS SOMETHING BAD IS GOING TO HAPPEN," SAID CORSX. WHOA.

BURN HIT THE BOOSTERS, TAKING OFF AS THEY BROKE THROUGH THE HARDENED ICE WALLS. SOON THEY WERE ALMOST BACK ON COURSE. BUT THE TREADS WERE STARTING TO LOOSEN ALONG WITH THE BULLDOZER SHIELD. THEY LOST ONE BULLDOZER SHIELD AND THEN THE NEXT ONE. THE LIGHTS WERE DANGLING AND BROKE OFF.

"WE MADE IT," SAID CORSX. "THERE IT IS, THAT GIANT WALL TRAP."

"OKAY," SAID BURN. "HERE WE GO, MAXIMUM POWER. WOOOOHOOOOOOO!"

THE TREADS BEGAN TO BREAK EVEN MORE UNDER THE TREMENDOUS STRAIN, BUT THEY WERE HOLDING TOGETHER AS THE ICE-TRAP WALLS CLOSED FASTER.

"WE MADE IT, BURN. YEAH. YOU SEE THAT? THAT BEAUTIFUL BLUE LIGHT?"

"THE BLUE LIGHTS." WE FINALLY MADE IT.

AS THEY WENT ON, SOMETHING BEGAN TO BOTHER THEM.

"WE'RE GETTING CLOSER, AND I DON'T SEE ANY MONSTERS," SAID CORSX.

THEN, FROM THE ICE-COLD SHADOWS, ICEZARDIANS POURED FORTH. THEY JUMPED ON THE SNOW VEHICLE, CAUSING IT TO

GO OUT OF CONTROL, BUT BEFORE THEY COULD GET TO CORSX, BURN HIT THE EJECT PANEL.

"MAKE IT, BUDDY, ALL THE WAY," SAID BURN, BLEEDING. "YAAHOOOOOOO! DON'T FORGET TO BE MACH WAY PASSED COOL"

THE SNOW VEHICLE FLEW OFF INTO THE COLD DEPTHS AS A HUGE CANYON APPEARED.

CORSX MADE IT TO A LARGE ALTAR. BUT THIS TIME, HE SPOTTED THE BLUE GEM ITSELF SITTING IN THE MIDDLE OF A HUGE DARK CENTER ON A PILLAR. THERE WAS NO BRIDGE ANYWHERE TO BE SEEN OR FOUND. CORSX USED HIS ROCKET HOOK TO SWING ACROSS THE ICE. THE ALTAR PILLAR WHERE THE BLUE JEWEL SAT WAS TOO SLIPPERY. HE ALMOST SLID PAST THE GEM. HE REGAINED HIS FOOTING BY USING HIS KNIFE, BUT IT BROKE ON THE ICE. CORSX THEN USED AN ENERGY BEAM BLAST TO SLOW HIMSELF AND PROPEL HIMSELF TOWARD THE JEWEL. HE GRABBED IT, AND THE TEMPLE FELL TO SNOW, CAUSING A HUGE PILLAR OF BLUE LIGHT TO PIERCE THE SKY.

* * *

THE OLD CARETAKER KNEW IT WAS TIME. ALL FIVE HAD BEEN FOUND, AND A RACE TO THE KING'S ROAD IT WOULD BE. WHO WOULD REACH IT? THE FORCES OF GOOD OR THE ATROCITIES OF EVIL—OR MAYBE A NEUTRAL PARTY—IN THE END WHO WOULD DECIDE THE OUTCOME OF PAGAMA.

* * *

BACK AT THE ICE CITADEL RUINS . . .

"HEY, STOP THE TRUCK," SAID CORSX.

THE TRUCK HIT CORSX. AS IT DID, HE JUST TURNED INTO SNOW. ZORBOR GOT OUT.

ZORBOR SNICKERED AND LAUGHED LIKE A WEASEL. "MUST FIND BLUE SPARKLY FOR MASTER."

"ZORBOR, WHY?" CORSX ASKED. HE LOOKED INTO HIS EYES, SEEING THAT ZORBOR WAS NOT HIMSELF.

ZORBOR LUNGED AT CORSX, BUT THE SNOW ROSE, HITTING HIM. CORSX WAS ASTOUNDED AT WHAT HAD JUST HAPPENED. A BLUE LIGHT ENGULFED THEM.

"AN ANCIENT EVIL," SAID CORSX. "THE VEIL OF THE NIGHT, THE EMPEROR OF ALL FLAME ALONG WITH A HIDEOUS SHADOW THAT THREATENS ALL. DARK OVERLORDS OF FIENDISH DEVILTRY. KING'S ROAD. THE ONE TRUE KING OF PAGAMA WHO SITS UPON THE THRONE OF THE KING. AN ETERNAL NIGHT, A NIGHT THAT NEVER ENDS. ONLY THE FIVE CAN END THE BEAST OF THE NIGHT. AN AGE OF BLACKEST PITCH."

THE LIGHT FADED, AND ZORBOR WAS GONE, ALONG WITH THE TRUCK. ONLY MOASSA REMAINED.

"MOASSA, ARE YOU ALL RIGHT? HANG ON."

CORSX USED ALL HIS MIGHT. HE SUMMONED AN ICE BIRD AND TOLD IT WHERE TO GO.

"I'M SORRY," SAID CORSX. "I CAN'T COME WITH YOU. I MUST HEAD FOR KING'S ROAD."

* * *

ELSEWHERE . . .

THE OLD CARETAKER SAID, "SO IT IS TIME FOR OUR KING TO BE DECIDED, EH? I HOPE HE OR SHE IS A GOOD ONE. YEP, YEP." HE CONTINUED SWEEPING THE FLOOR.

CORSX LOG ENDS . . .

* * *

PAGAMA CASTLE LOG BEGINS . . .

CHRONICLE LOG

PAGAMA CASTLE

CONTINUED

(FLYING) HAGGLESBEE SAID, "I MANAGED TO USE MOST OF MY WIND POWERS, AND MOST OF ALL, I CAN BE THE WIND ITSELF. BUT THIS DRAINS MY LIFE, SO I HAVE TO BE CAUTIOUS ABOUT WHEN AND HOW I USE IT. BUT THE GREATEST GIFT IS FLIGHT. I CAN SENSE SO MANY SOUND VIBRATIONS, SMELL SO MANY SCENTS."

HAGGLESBEE TOOK OFF AT SUPER SPEED. BEFORE HE KNEW IT, HE WAS AT THE HOUSE OF THE PAGAMA LORD. THE DRAWBRIDGE LOWERED AS THE OLD CARETAKER APPEARED.

"I AM THE BEARER OF THE RUBY OF THE WIND," SAID HAGGLESBEE. "I HAVE RETURNED, OLD CARETAKER."

CHUCKLING, THE OLD CARETAKER SAID, "THE POWER OF THE WIND. THE POWER OF FLIGHT, THE POWER OF STORMS. WHAT A DESTRUCTIVE OR HEALING FORCE. BUT . . . UH-OH, DO YOU SENSE THAT, BEARER?"

"SO ANOTHER HAS ARRIVED," SAID HAGGLESBEE.

"YES, FOLLOW ME," SAID THE OLD CARETAKER.

THEY BEGAN TO WALK THE HALLS OF THE KING, GOING THROUGH THE ENORMOUS CORRIDORS UNTIL THEY REACHED A HIDDEN CAVERN BENEATH THE CASTLE.

THE OLD CARETAKER SAID, "THIS IS THE POOL OF RADIANCE. IT IS SAID THAT HERE, GREAT WATERS OF HEALING AND MYSTERIOUS POWER ONCE FLOWED."

AS HE SPOKE, SOMEONE ROSE FROM THE WATER.

"I AM THE BEARER OF THE RUBY OF WATER," SAID CORSX. "I SEEK THE KING'S THRONE."

"YOU SURVIVED THE TRIALS BUT . . ." SAID HAGGLESBEE.

"SO, YOU BEAR WIND, HUH? WELL, WATER VERSUS WIND," SAID CORSX, SMIRKING.

"I AM A MAN OF PEACE, WATER. I DO NOT SEEK WAR," SAID HAGGLESBEE.

"WHAT KIND OF WARRIOR ARE YOU? HUH?" ASKED CORSX.

THE OLD CARETAKER INTERRUPTED. "UH-OH, HMM."

HAGGLESBEE AND CORSX BOTH SENSED ANOTHER PRESENCE.

"THIS IS THE SMITHY HERE," EXPLAINED THE OLD CARETAKER. "GREAT WEAPONS OF VICTORY HAVE BEEN FORGED."

"HOW DID IT GET SO HOT IN HERE?" ASKED HAGGLESBEE, WIPING HIS HEAD.

"I AM THE BEARER OF FLAME," SAID A VOICE. "I AM THE BEARER OF THE RUBY OF FIRE. I AM IGNEOUS, YOUR EMPEROR. BOW BEFORE ME, LOWLY WORMS OF THE DUST, OR DIE A HORRIBLE, SCORCHING DEATH."

"HOLD UP," SAID CORSX. "LAST TIME I CHECKED, WATER BEATS FIRE. THAT IS UNLESS YOU LIKE STEAM BATHS."

"WIND BEATS FIRE," ADDED HAGGLESBEE. HE WAS WATCHING IGNEOUS'S BODY MOVEMENTS CAREFULLY.

IGNEOUS SAID, "IF THE FLAMES ARE TOO HOT, EVEN WATER EVAPORATES. A WIND ONLY SPREADS A FLAME, MAKING IT BIGGER. BOY! HUMPH YOU ARE BUT MERE CHILDREN BEFORE A GOD!"

"THE RAGE IN YOUR EYES TELLS ME THAT YOU ARE ONLY EXCITED BY DESTRUCTION AND WAR," SAID CORSX. "FOR YOU TO BECOME KING WOULD ONLY MEAN ANOTHER TYRANT, JUST LIKE BEFORE."

HE JUST POWERED UP. I BETTER WATCH OUT, OR IT COULD BE OVER IN ONE STRIKE, THOUGHT HAGGLESBEE.

IGNEOUS POWERED UP AND WAS ABOUT TO UNLEASH HIS RAGE WHEN ALL OF A SUDDEN . . .

THE OLD CARETAKER SPOKE UP. "LOOKS LIKE ANOTHER ONE HAS COME FOR THE THRONE. WELL, IT'S TO BE EXPECTED, AFTER ALL."

EVERYONE SAID, "HMMMMMMMM."

THEY HEADED FOR THE GARDEN, ONLY TO HEAR AN EERIE, DEAD LAUGHTER RISE UP.

"I AM GRAIL RA, DARK SORCERER. I BEAR THE POWER OF EARTH, LET ALONE MY DARK ARTS." HE LAUGHED UNDER HIS HOOD. "SO NOW, ALL ARE HERE."

IGNEOUS SHOUTED, "I'VE HAD ENOUGH!"

IGNEOUS LET LOOSE A HUGE RING OF FLAME, BUT GRAIL RA MELTED INTO THE DIRT, CORSX TURNED INTO WATER, AND HAGGLESBEE FLEW.

IGNEOUS TOOK OFF, USING HIS HEAT, AND CHASED AFTER HAGGLESBEE. HE TRIED TO USE HIS WIND POWER TO BLOW OUT HIS FLAME, BUT IGNEOUS CHANGED THE AREA TO SCORCHING TEMPERATURES. CORSX TORE UP THE GROUND,

TRYING TO HIT GRAIL RA, BUT HE APPEARED BEHIND CORSX FIRING OFF BLACK BALLS OF ENERGY IN HIS DIRECTION. CORSX DODGED, SLIDING ACROSS THE GROUND, BUT HUGE EARTH HANDS APPEARED OVER HIM, SMASHING HIM. HE TURNED INTO WATER AND MANAGED TO ESCAPE. THEN, USING WATER KNIVES AND WATER BLADES, HE CAUGHT GRAIL RA, CUTTING HIS ARM OFF.

MEANWHILE . . .

IGNEOUS SHOT FLAME BALLS AT HAGGLESBEE AND THEN USED FLAMING SLASH KICKS IN MIDAIR, ALONG WITH A FLAMING SWORD ATTACK. HAGGLESBEE DODGED BUT STILL GOT BURNED FALLING DOWN FROM THE SKY AT GREAT SPEEDS. HE CAUGHT HIMSELF AS IGNEOUS CONTINUED HIS RELENTLESS ATTACK. HAGGLESBEE MANAGED TO GET FAR ENOUGH AWAY FROM HIM TO CREATE A HUGE WIND VORTEX THAT BEGAN TO SUCK IGNEOUS IN. HE SHOT OFF AN ENORMOUS FLAME, BUT IT WAS EXTINGUISHED. HAGGLESBEE MANEUVERED THE WIND TO THE GROUND, BUT FROM BEHIND HIM, GRAIL RA APPEARED HITTING HIT HIM IN THE BACK WITH A ROCK. THEN, HE USED A BLACK-BOLT SPELL. HAGGLESBEE FELL TO HIS KNEES AS CORSX SLASHED GRAIL RA IN TWO. IGNEOUS WAS INFURIATED AS HE ROSE TO HIS FEET, AND HIS EYES GREW BLOOD RED. HE LET LOOSE A BARRAGE OF WHITE FLAMES THAT BEGAN MELTING THE AREA. CORSX WAS TRYING TO PUT IT OUT, BUT HIS WATER EVAPORATED. AS A LAST ATTEMPT,

HAGGLESBEE TRIED TO SET UP A WIND BARRIER, BUT THAT WAS BLOWN UP TOO.

"FLAME BEATS ALL!" IGNEOUS ROARED WITH MIGHTY WHITE-HOT FLAMES IGNITING AROUND HIM.

"I SAVE OR TRY, AND THIS IS WHAT I GET," SAID CORSX, SMIRKING. HE WAS HURT AND LYING ON THE GROUND.

"NOW I WILL ASCEND THE KING'S THRONE," SAID IGNEOUS. "FOR I AM NO MERE KING; I AM AN EMPEROR."

GRAIL RA LAUGHED. "PLEASE YOU EMPEROR, WHAT A CLOWN."

THE EARTH ROSE TO COVER IGNEOUS. HE BURNED IT UP, BUT GRAIL RA CONTINUED HIS ASSAULT.

"EARTH COVERS FIRE, EXTINGUISHING IT," SAID GRAIL RA.

LAUGHING, IGNEOUS SAID, "WHITE FLAME IS NOT MY FULL MIGHT. THERE IS MORE BEYOND THIS FLAME. SO BEAR WITNESS TO MY—"

IGNEOUS FELL, KNOCKED OUT. GRAIL RA APPEARED BEHIND HIM AND BEGAN CHOKING HIM.

GRAIL RA SAID, "MAGIC IS GOOD BUT OLD-FASHIONED; BONEY HANDS BEAT ALL." HE LAUGHED AS HE CHOKED

IGNEOUS. "NOW, I SHALL CONSUME ALL OF YOUR RUBIES FOR MY OWN." (HE CAST A SOUL-SEPARATION SPELL).

THEIR RUBY ESSENCES WERE BEING EXTRACTED FROM THEM.

THE OLD CARETAKER SAID, "I WANTED TO WAIT UNTIL LIGHT APPEARS. BUT THIS IS SO INTERESTING."

THE FIGHT TOOK THEM FROM THE GARDEN TO THE SMITHY AND FROM THERE TO THE WEAPONS HALL, THE BANQUET HALL, AND FINALLY THE CASTLE CRYPT.

THE OLD CARETAKER CHUCKLED. "UH-OH, LIGHT."

"GRAIL IMPERIUM, ULTIMATE CHARGE."

A HUGE ARMADA OF LIGHT KNIGHTS CHARGED FORWARD IN A BARRAGE OF ENERGY, HITTING GRAIL RA.

"THE LIGHT!" YELLED GRAIL RA. "THE LIGHT! NO, I HATE THE LIGHT! GET AWAY FROM ME." HE BURNED UP. "NOOOOO!" HE SCREAMED IN PAIN.

GRAIL RA FELL, SMOKING AND HURT. HE DID NOT MOVE.

"ALL FIVE ARE HERE AT LAST. I AM THE BEARER OF LIGHT. I AM SAMANTHA ALROUS CRYSTALA, PRINCESS OF DESERNA.

MY FRIEND CLOCKWORK KNIGHT LEFT HIS LEGACY TO ME. I TAKE UP THE GRAIL IMPERIUM LANCE BLADE."

THE OLD CARETAKER SAID, "MA'AM, THE KING'S THRONE AWAITS THEE."

SAMANTHA SAID, "THE LIGHT HAS TOLD ME OF IGNEOUS'S DARK AMBITIONS AND OF GRAIL RA'S TREACHERY. NOW, I TAKE THE LEAD. "TORLOC XHIOC ROC NO TORE!"

IN AN INSTANT, THE GEMS APPEARED AS EACH ONE BEGAN TO DRAIN AWAY FROM THEM. THE LOOM RUBIES APPEARED BEFORE SAMANTHA. THE OLD CARETAKER ESCORTED HER TO THE KING'S HALL. THEY WALKED THE HALLS FINALLY APPROACHING THE BARRIER SURROUNDING THE KING'S THRONE.

THE OLD CARETAKER SAID, "GO ON, YOUNG GIRL. APPROACH WHAT IS NOW YOUR DESTINY. CLAIM YOUR RADIANCE, AND USHER US INTO AN AGE OF PLATINUM."

SAMANTHA ALROUS CRYSTALA APPROACHED THE KING'S THRONE WITH THE FOUR JEWELS SHINING. AN ILLUMINATING LIGHT EMERGED AS FOUR BEAMS SHOT OUT, PENETRATING THE BARRIER, THEN THE FIFTH JEWEL OF LIGHT BEAM SHOT OUT. THE KING'S BARRIER WAS GONE.

"NOW, THE THRONE WILL JUDGE YOU, DEEMING YOU WORTHY," SAID THE OLD CARETAKER.

A LIGHT ENGULFED HER, DRAWING HER CLOSER. THE LOOM RUBIES BEGAN TO COME TOGETHER AS ONE. THE SYMBOL OF LOOM APPEARED AROUND HER. THERE WAS A MAJESTIC LIGHT, AND THEN ALL OF A SUDDEN, A BLAST OF DARK ENERGY HIT HER, MAKING HER FALL TO THE GROUND UNCONSCIOUS.

DIABOLICAL LAUGHTER RANG OUT. "AT LAST, I SHALL ASCEND THE KING'S THRONE RULING ON HIGH AS A GOD." THE EVIL LAUGHTER RESUMED.

THE OLD CARETAKER SAT UPON THE KING'S THRONE, ABSORBING ITS GREAT OVERWHELMING POWER. THE OLMGALA CRYSTAL WAS MERGING WITH THE CARETAKER.

"AS THE OLD SAYING GOES, CAN'T KEEP A DEAD MAN OR THING DOWN, EH?" SAID A VOICE.

AN ANCIENT DISPEL SEAL BLAST SHOT OUT, HITTING THE CARETAKER WHICH MADE HIM FALL FROM THE THRONE. THE PERSON MOVED FAST AND SOON HELD THE OLMGALA CRYSTAL.

"SO THIS IS THE GREAT AND MAGNIFICENT OLMGALA. SO NOW, I HOLD THE SACRED POWER ALONG WITH THE STAR BUSTER, THE M CLEAVER, AND THE MIGHT OF A GOD."

"SO YOU, MIKITA W," SAID THE OLD CARETAKER.

"NOPE, NOT HIM, BUT I KNOW YOU, FORTUNE-TELLER, DARK SPIRIT. WHY ARE YOU HERE, AND HOW DID YOU RETURN?"

FORTUNE-TELLER SPOKE IN A DEEP, ANCIENT, DECAYING VOICE. "NO THANKS TO YOU. BUT SHE SAW FIT TO BESTOW HER MAJESTIC GRACE UPON ME."

HER. SO SHE HAS BEGUN TO MOVE, HUH?
"WELL, FORTUNE-TELLER, I HAVE USE OF THIS CRYSTAL, SEE."

THE FORTUNE-TELLER SAID, "YOU DARE ROB ME OF THE KING'S THRONE AND GODHOOD. YOU WILL PAY FOR THIS. YOU WILL PAY!"

SHE MUST BE GREATLY WEAKENED TO NEED A NEW HEART. "HEY, FORTUNE-TELLER, IF SHE FREED YOU FROM AN ULTIMATE OBLIVION OF NONEXISTENCE, HOW COME YOU WERE ABOUT TO GAIN THE POWER OF A GOD? THE OLD DOUBLE CROSS, EH? LOOKS LIKE A NEW GOD WON'T BE BORN THIS DAY OR ANY OTHER. I SHOULD END YOU LIKE BEFORE." A VOICE SAID

THEN CORSX AND HAGGLESBEE RAN INTO THE THRONE ROOM ONLY TO SEE THE CARETAKER, SAMANTHA, AND THE MYSTERIOUS PERSON.

CORSX ASKED, "CARETAKER?"

THE MYSTERIOUS PERSON USED A SPELL BREAK TO END THE CHARADE. NOW THEY TOO SAW THE TRUTH.

HAGGLESBEE SAID, "THE SCOURGE OF ALL PAGAMA—FORTUNE-TELLER, THE DARK ONE."

FORTUNE-TELLER LAUGHED. "ANOTHER TIME, PHANTOM. ANOTHER TIME."

FORTUNE-TELLER VANISHED WITH SAMANTHA.

ANGRY AND STUNNED, THEY SAID TOGETHER, "SAMANTHA!"

PHANTOM SAID, "TO THE SOUTHEAST IS A DARK TOWER CALLED TERRA. THAT'S WHERE YOU'LL FIND THAT DECREPIT FOSSIL. OH WAIT! YOU'LL NEED SOME POWERS TO FIGHT BACK, SO HERE."

PHANTOM THREW THE OLMGALA CRYSTAL INTO THE AIR THEN USED THE STAR BUSTER TO SHATTER IT BACK INTO ITS SEPARATE STATE.

CORSX SAID, "I GET THE EARTH RUBY THIS TIME. WELL . . . I GET TO SEE WHAT I CAN DO WITH THIS."

HAGGLESBEE SAID, "I GET THE FIRE RUBY THIS TIME AND THE POWER OF FLAME." (LET'S SEE IF I CAN HANDLE THE POWER OF FLAME, THOUGHT HAGGLESBEE.)

PHANTOM "I HAVE OTHER MATTERS TO ATTEND TO. OH AND GIVE THE REMAINING TWO TO SOMEONE YOU TRUST." (HE'S CLOSE AT LAST; I FOUND HIM). "OH, ONE MORE THING, IF YOU CAN'T BEAT FORTUNE-TELLER, THEN THIS PLANET HAS NO FUTURE BECAUSE IT'S BEGINNING TO BREAK APART. THE RUBIES ARE NEEDED AT THE TOWER OF TERRA TO STABILIZE THE PLANET."

THE TWO TOOK OFF AND LEFT THE CASTLE. MEANWHILE, PHANTOM WENT DEEPER INTO THE CASTLE TO FIND WHAT HE WAS LOOKING FOR.

KING'S LOG ENDS . . .

TERRA LOG BEGINS . . .

CHRONICLE LOG

Tower of Terra

TOWER OF TERRA

A rescue chopper thundered through the sky headed southeast toward an unexplored part of the planet Pagama.

"Evil is an ever-mysterious entity that consumes and corrupts, as its hunger is never ending," Corsx said, a tired tone in his voice. He was leaning his head on the window, staring out.

"Evil?" said Hagglesbee. "The power of the flame is within me now. That other guy couldn't handle it. Maybe I can." He folded his hands.

"You had the power of wind," said Corsx. "Now, you have fire, I had water and now earth."

"Hey, man," said the pilot, "These storm winds are getting nuts." *Yikes*.

Rock Gear Hound said, "Hey, Corsx, bud. So this ruby is water, and I get to use it, huh? Wonder what I can do with it. How'd it work for you, Corsx?"

Norsunma said, "I have wind, now we must save light. So we must get to this tower, use the rubies to stabilize the planet, and then beat that dark creature from a bygone age."

"Should be all in a day's work for us, huh? I mean, we can do it right?" said Corsx.

And so our adventurers go forth into the darkness and the unknowns of Terra.

That was fifty-five days ago . . .

*   *   *

Present day and time . . .

"I've been on the road for days now. Barely sleeping and eating. It's been chasing me for days . . . months even . . . how much longer can I hold out? When we got here, it was a paradise with all the trimmings. After the big one years ago, all of a sudden, the planet Pagama reformed and we, the few survivors, began our trek back home," said Burn.

The snow vehicle was tossed about as it flew all over the jagged terrain. Broken ice pillars pierced the hull; soon, air began to seep in. As it did, Burn heard a loud, high-pitched screeching. His eyes darted nervously, looking at his meters and gauges.

Looking around and breathing hard, Burn said, "It's coming!" His hands shook. "Crap! Come on! Move, please! Please move!" He was shaking even more. He hit the gas, and the ignition started. He thundered on into the bone-chilling night.

"Checkpoint," said Burn. "I got to rendezvous with everyone quickly. I got to keep going. Maybe, just maybe, there are others left. There just have to be. There have to be."

His eyes got heavy. "We're getting the heck out of here . . . *alive.*

The End—or Is It Just the Beginning?

HEART
OF
THE DRAGON

Every harvest, our village holds a ceremony where ten of us kids leave the village for as long as the harvest lasts.

This is my story. My name is . . .

Tayo

*   *   *

From afar, the clouds part, revealing to us a fruitful landscape covered in lush greenery. The harvest begins, bringing new life, which is important to the people's and the land's survival. As we glide across the land, we see a boy looking into the sky daydreaming.

This young boy's name is Tayo. Tayo looks to the sky and then closes his eyes.

He hears the wind whistle over the grassy plains. Tayo hears a faint voice calling his name. It's his friend Shiruumi.

"Tayo, where are you? Can you hear me? Are you sleeping again or daydreaming?"

Tayo opens his eyes and sees Shiruumi smiling over him.

"Tayo, hurry! The harvest!" says Shiruumi. "The ceremony is starting. They're handing out the Belts of the Heart."

This belt is used to put the collected emblems into place when they are awarded.

Tayo says, "Oh no."

He jumps up and runs down the hill only to end up tripping. Shiruumi runs after him with her arms up. She is excited. Tayo hits the river and frog-jumps his way out. Ochum, the old farmer, can see Tayo.

"Tayo," says Ochum, "you must hurry or you'll miss the chance you have waited for and then another year will pass for you."

Tayo hurries as best he can on to the village square soaking wet. The villagers see Tayo. They giggle but the elder Seychinrai thumps his cane on the ground. The villagers grow silent.

Seychinrai speaks in an old, deep, wise voice. "We have been blessed yet again with a bountiful harvest. Now once again, the harvest ceremony begins. Step forward, young ones."

Ten children, both boys and girls, step forward.

The last two children chosen are Tayo and Xi Fung.

Xi Fung says, "So, Tayo, we were chosen as well this year." He laughs softly with a serious face.

Tayo looks at him and feels scared but doesn't know why.

"See you tomorrow, Tayo," says Xi Fung.

That night, at dinner, Tayo sits with his family and eats his favorite dish: noodles and beef.

Tayo's mom, Moon Sing, is a beautiful woman. Hau Mung, his father, is a farmer and a hard worker.

Then there's Moon Si and Mau Ru, Tayo's baby brother and sister.

Moon Sing says, "Tayo, what's wrong? You're not eating. I fixed what you like the most."

Hau Mung says, "Come with me, Tayo."

"Yes, Father," says Tayo.

They walk outside and look up at the stars in the sky.

Hau Mung says, "Tayo, the time has come for you to—"

"Father, I . . ." Tayo begins nervously.

"Yes, my son?" says Hau Mung.

"I won't let you down. I know I sleep in the field. But I can hear the dragon calling me," says Tayo.

"The dragon, Tayo?" He looks at his son with concern. "Come on, Tayo; your mom fixed some dessert."

They go back to the house. Tayo's mom and dad talk to each other as the children sleep.

Moon Sing says, "I'm worried, Hau Mung; it's just like you, Grandpa, and my father."

"I know, but it is up to Tayo to choose," says Hau Mung.

HEART

In the morning, the children set out. Each one has ten days to complete the task that was handed to them.

"Sure is hot today, oh man," says Tayo. He looks up toward the sun.

Tayo wipes his head beginning his travels down the long, dusty road. It's hot and humid as he continues through the dry land. An autumn day passes as Tayo notices how much the area changes when he travels away from his village because his village is lush with greenery and plentiful with water.

Tayo is resting in the shade of a tree. All of a sudden, an old woman appears, or rather Tayo didn't see her on the other side of the tree. The old woman speaks to Tayo and tells him her name.

Shy Vey says, "Hello, young man. Oh, I see the harvest ceremony begins again. Will you be kind enough to help me?"

"I'm Tayo," he says.

"Tayo, a strong name, it means 'heart of the dragon.'"

Tayo carries the old woman across the river on his back, even though it takes him off his path.

"Thank you, young Tayo," she says. "Oh, I hear you youngsters were looking for the crest of the heart. Do you have any idea where it is, young one?"

"Do you know where it is?" asks Tayo.

"Yes, here you go," says the old woman.

"The crest of the heart! But how?" asks Tayo.

"My son traveled the road and the land; he came across it as he too once entered the harvest festival. He used to live in your village."

"Thanks a lot, ma'am. I really appreciate this. Thank you."
He is excited.

"Be well, young Tayo. Be well," she says.

Tayo has completed his first trial, the trial of the heart. Though he did not want to because it took him off of his path, he took the time to help someone as his mother and father had taught him.

SOUL

Tayo's quest continues. Now, Tayo faces a new challenge.

Qui Soon says, "Hey, Tayo, I completed my second trial. The trial of water."

"What is it?" Tayo asks eagerly.

Qui Soon laughs. "Find out for yourself, Tayo."

Qui Soon continues to laugh as he walks away from Tayo.

Tayo becomes angry, but he calms down. He then enters the ancient water ruins.

"Hello? Is anyone there? Hello?" calls Tayo.

As Tayo walks forward, he sees an old man sitting on the back of a turtle. The old man tells Tayo his name.

Ty Fong says, "Welcome, young one."

"I am Tayo Moon Xi. I come—"

"The test of water, eh?" says Ty Fong, rubbing his beard. "Young Tayo, I am not the test master. This is just where I live, but I hear the test of water is hard. It's through that door. I'll watch your things."

The old man pushes Tayo then steals his things.

Tayo falls through the door, and it closes behind him. Tayo wanders the damp corridors until he sees a huge pit with waterfall columns all around. Then, all of a sudden, a huge gush of water hits Tayo. From behind him, the old man appears once more.

Ty Fong laughs. "Well now, Tayo, glad you could come. If you want this pouch back, beat the test of water."

A turtle appears under Tayo as he floats in the water.

Ty Fong smacks his knee. "Now, ma boy, it's a race to see who can get to the end and the pouch. Let's see what you got, kiddo. Maybe some of yer mom's dumplings are in there." He licks his lips.

"Did Qui Soon do this test too? Whoa."

A huge gate made of bricks suddenly drops. Ty Fong prepares himself. Tayo prepares his feet as well. The race begins, and Tayo's turtle explodes in a burst of speed. Ty Fong is taking the stance of stone, firm and anchored. His turtle is ahead of Tayo, as they speed through the straights, twists, turns, curves, and loop de loops. They reach a huge corkscrew in the path, Ty Fong explodes in a massive burst of both speed and force. Tayo falls behind drastically.

Ty Fong laughs. "Ho, ho, ho! What's wrong, youngster? Heh, heh, heh."

Tayo says, "I have to catch up, but how?"

Then Tayo remembers something his grandmother told him.

Sing Moon Lai told him once, "Tayo, my grandson, water is like our souls—ever-changing and flowing in path energy. Ultimately leading to the path of the dragon."

Tayo opens his eyes, and a great burst of speed erupts. He takes a downward spiral corkscrew, then almost near the end, Tayo and the giant turtle jump before the water ends. They fly over Ty Fong's head appearing in front of him. Tayo sees the light up ahead, and he passes the finish line.

He continues on grabbing his pouch as he sails on the turtle's back. Ty Fong stops and watches Tayo as he sails away. He turns around and goes back into the cave . . .

When Tayo looks in his bag, he sees the soul emblem next to the heart emblem.

Tayo has passed the water trial. What will he face next?

BODY

Tayo sails down the river and goes ashore. He says his good-bye to the turtle.

"Where am I now?" asks Tayo. "Boy, am I hungry!"

As Tayo gets ready to sit, he sees Tung Mai. She is covered in dirt and mud.

"Tayo, is that you? Long time, no see. I just finished the earth test, but I didn't win. It's a doozy. Good luck." Said Tung Mai.

Tayo says, "Thanks! Are you okay, Tung Mai? You look hurt."

"Just tired; that's all. I'm full of youthful energy." She giggles.

Tayo enters the earth temple. As he walks around the place, he sees huge stone statues.

"Wowwww! Hellooooo!" says Tayo.

A woman appears from the dojo and tells Tayo her name.

Ai Shi says, "Welcome, young harvester. You are here to help me dig, right?" She smiles at him.

"Dig? Uh no, I came for the—"

Ai Shi interrupts him. "Yep, you're here to dig. Let's go. Tayo, you say that's what they call you?"

Tayo follows her to a huge pit.

Ai Shi says, "I've been trying to dig to the other side to make a path because it's too long to go around. I'm glad you're here to help me."

"Where do I start?" asks Tayo. "But after this, I have to find—"

"The temple master, he took the long road around; it takes about fourteen days to and from, plenty of time to dig a path to the other side, right?" Ai Shi says and smiles.

Tayo's mouth drops open. "Sure."

He whistles a long time as he looks at the pit. "Well, let's get started, Ai Shi."

Tayo picks up his shovel and hits the rock, but he falls back. He gets up hitting the rock angrily.

Ai Shi giggles. "No, Tayo, like this."

She hits the rock at the right angle, breaking it apart. Tayo looks on in amazement, and the work continues. She breaks them with ease while he continues to struggle.

Night falls upon the land, and he wants to continue to work by candlelight. But Ai Shi stops him.

Tayo says, "I'm not getting tired, Ai Shi. I think I'm getting the hang of it."

Ai Shi responds, "Look, Tayo, the stars are out tonight. We can rest now and laugh. Remember, tomorrow's another day. Right, Tayo?"

She looks and sees Tayo asleep.

In the morning, he goes to wash up. As he lets the warm water hit his face, he remembers his grandfather Mu Quai.

Mu Quai says in a deep, bold voice, "Tayo, see these rocks in the quarry. They are relentless, strong, and anchored deep in Mother Earth. No matter what comes against them, they stand tall. But . . ."

"But?" prompts Tayo.

"But the great, anchored rock can be destroyed. Remember, Tayo, hot and cold, hot and cold," Mu Quai says.

Tayo jumps out of the water, throws his clothes on, and heads out of the earth temple. He flies past Ai Shi so quickly she thinks he is a ghost.

"Now I understand what he meant!" says Tayo. "Hot and cold."

Tayo uses a sword he saw in the dojo shack to cut down the bamboo trees. Next, he makes a long trench when he cuts the bamboo in two. He carefully connects them by using some rope he had from the dojo shack. When it is done, it is connected to the temple where they were digging.

Tayo takes the giant fan that was inside the temple's kitchen, which is used to prepare meals and warm the temple at night. When he puts these objects together, they create a huge wind machine like a hose. The bamboo ends, and the water falls into a huge metal pool where it is heated.

Tayo says, "Ai Shi, watch."

Tayo jumps up and down on the fan blower mechanism, and it shoots out a blast of hot water, steaming up the cave. Ai Shi jumps up and down on the pump next to the hot-water pump. When she does that, it shoots out a blast of cold water that begins to crack and break the rock, but without an escape route, the mud and slurry have no place to go.

Ai Shi says, "Tayo, stop!"

She's walking through the muddy water, which is up to her knees.

Tayo is excited and not paying attention. "Why?"

Ai Shi warns, "You're going to bring the cave down on our heads, Tayo, if this keeps up. I like your machine but—"

"I understand. Sorry!" He walks away disappointed.

As Tayo is eating his lunch, he sees a squirrel running around a tree, and it hits him—an idea, not the squirrel. Tayo works to redesign his machine so that it shoots the water at a controlled level. So it can be adjusted. He tests the controls, and it begins to cut into the rock. When he turns up the setting, it blasts out, creating a huge drilling motion. The farther the water blasts, the deeper they go, setting up wooden planks to hold up the cave tunnel and creating a solid and firm foundation.

Ai Shi says, "Tayo, I'm impressed! You moved earth."

Tayo is tired. "Yeah, I didn't think I had it in me."

Ai Shi says, "Tayo, the other side! You did it. I don't know what I'm going to tell the master when he gets back. But at least we can get to the other side now. Aww, he's sleeping."

When Tayo wakes up, he is on the other side of the mountain with his pouch. The path he dug is gone but how?

"How'd I get into town?" he asks.

"Ai Shi must have brought me but how? Huh, what's this? Whoaaaa, it's the . . ."

Tayo has passed the earth trial and has gained the body emblem. Earth unfaltering has been moved, not by power alone, but by knowledge as well . . .

Now there is but one more trial ahead for Tayo, and only three days left to make it home.

MIND

"Ai Shi, thank you," says Tayo. "Three down, one to go and only three days left to get back in time for the harvest festival."

As Tayo leaves his room, he sees a familiar yet cold face.

Xi Fung says, "Well, well, well, Tayo, you made it this far. I'm surprised you didn't run home and hide."

Tayo looks at Xi Fung's heart belt; it holds different emblems, including the ones he has already obtained.

"Oh these," says Xi Fung. "These are the emblems I gained after I finished those ridiculous children's games they call trials. Earth, wind, water, fire, power—I'll become the dragon this year."

Tayo says, "Wind, power, fire? I did the heart, body, water. Only one left, Xi Fung."

Xi Fung responds, "Heart? Please!" He waves his hand arrogantly. "Well, Tayo, see you later . . . Probably not." He laughs.

Tayo goes outside and sits down. He notices a child looking sad.

"What's wrong?" he asks. "I'm Tayo."

The child tells him his name.

Qao Chu says, "I lost my dolly, and I'm scared to go get it."

"Leave it to big brother Tayo, okay, Qao Chu?"

Qao Chu smiles.

When they get to where he lost his doll, Tayo is amazed.

"You lost it in here?" Tayo says. "This is a demon's cave, but okay, I'll help you. Just hold on to this rope, so I can come back out, okay, Qao Chu?"

Qao Chu nods. "Right, Big Brother."

Without hesitation, Tayo goes into the cave. It's deep, dark, moist crevasses lure Tayo deeper. He slides down a path that leads him to a giant door, as he goes deeper, Tayo feels heat. He can see light ahead and follows it only to find out he's in a volcano. He's sweating and can barely breathe or see. His vision is getting blurry.

Tayo calls back, "I can't go on. It's too hot. Sorry, Qao Chu." He faints.

When he wakes up, it's cool and dark.

"Huh, where am I?" he wonders.

A monk introduces himself to Tayo as Shao Ko.

"Greetings, young one," says the monk. "I see the harvest festival continues. I passed that village many moons ago. So what brings you here?"

"I'm Tayo. A kid named Qao Chu dropped his doll. I came in here to look for it, but I slipped and fell deeper. Now I'm here, Shao Ko."

Shao Ko says, "Did you find the doll by any chance, Tayo?"

"No, not yet," says Tayo.

"Well, I saw something shining as I came down . . . or rather up. Let's go, okay?"

Tayo and Shao Ko go upward past the jagged rock formations and the heated vents that blow hot steam. As Tayo and Shao Ko progress further, they begin to see something shiny. Tayo gets closer and sees the doll's button eye glimmering at him. All of a sudden, the volcano begins to erupt.

"Oh no!" Tayo shouts, afraid.

Shao Ko is calm. "Tayo he calls."

Tayo recalls something from when he was knocked out.

He is talking to his mother as they walk.

Moon Sing says, "Tayo, you have a strong mind; never let it waver. Always see using your mind's eye."

"Mind's eye?" asks Tayo.

Moon Sing says, "Yes, Tayo, the eye that can see through tricks and deception. The mind plays tricks on you sometimes, my son. Remember to be calm and see the truth."

Tayo opens his eyes and touches the doll.

Tayo says, "I was nervous and scared; that was just rumbling off in the distance, Shao Ko."

Shao Ko and Tayo emerge from the volcano. But now there's no smoke coming from it. The area is silent.

Shao Ko says, "So, Tayo, young harvester, I see you have all four emblems."

"All four?" He gives him a confused look.

Tayo feels something inside the doll. It was the mind emblem. "See what is not there; the illusion of the mind breaks through it with the eye of truth."

Tayo moves down the roadway and sees a cloaked person selling apples.

"I am but a teller of grand fortunes, my boy; I can see this is not the path for you. Return home, and choose another path. Here, take this fruit; it will give you strength."

Tayo says, "Um, thanks, uh . . ."

Tayo drops the fruit and looks up. The person is gone, as if he or she never existed.

BALANCE

Shao Ko leads Tayo to the Temple of the Dragon's gates.

Tayo says, "Shao Ko?"

"Beware, Tayo," warns Shao Ko. "Beware."

He walks off into the sunset as Tayo enters the path of the dragon. When he gets to the Temple of the Dragon, he sees an old, run-down place.

"This is the Temple of the Dragon?" he asks.

Xi Fung looks angry. "Yes, how disappointing to travel so far to gain nothing."

"Gain nothing?" repeats Tayo.

"Yes, nothing," says Xi Fung. "It's just me and you; the others failed or rather . . ."

Tayo says, "You hurt them? Why?"

"Because I desire the power to do what I want," answers Xi Fung. "The power of the dragon. That's why I went along with this stupid joke of a contest, but it was a waste."

Xi Fung didn't learn anything, but I did: mind, body, soul, and heart, not earth, water, wind, and fire.

"I see now."

Xi Fung angrily replies "See what? Tayo, what are you babbling about? I never liked you; that's why I bullied you. You were beneath me."

"I always tried to be your friend," says Tayo. "But you always acted superior. Then, as we got older, you began to bully me. Now I see you are the one who is weak."

Xi Fung becomes enraged. "How dare you!" he shouts. "I'm better than you, and I'll prove it now, you loser. I'm going to enjoy hurting you. All this time, I held myself back but no more!"

"I see, Xi Fung. This is who you really are," says Tayo.

Tayo remembers something that the elder told him.

Seychinrai says, "I see that Xi Fung bullies you, Tayo. Shall I talk to him?"

"No, sir," Said Tayo

"I see in your eyes your reason," the elder says. "Xi Fung desires power perhaps because he did not have a family of his own, but he chooses to walk the path of the dragon. Sadly, like so many before him, he seeks greed, power, and arrogance. This will be his undoing."

"I understand, sir. I understand," Tayo responds in a sad tone.

It begins to rain in the Temple of the Dragon. Thunder and lightning crash down to the earth.

The elder was right about him, thinks Tayo.

"Xi Fung, stop. Please, it does not have to be this way."

"I seek to destroy what is in front of me, and that is you, Tayo. Oh, think of all the wonderful things I'll do with the power of the dragon." Shouted Xi Fung.

"Very well. If this is what you want, but I will not let such a thing fall into your hands," says Tayo.

Xi Fung attacks Tayo, but Tayo dodges him.

Be as the soul, always flowing toward the path of the dragon.

Xi Fung roundhouses and misses Tayo then jump-kicks falling to the ground missing him again as Tayo dodges.

Be as the body; move the stronger anchored foe, Tayo tells himself.

Xi Fung uses his venom-strike technique to attack Tayo. He dodges, and then Xi Fung throws dirt in his face.

The illusion of the eyes—be mindful of the truth; see with the eye of the dragon.

Xi Fung goes to kick him in the chest and misses. Tayo uses his sash, and the more Xi Fung attacks, the more he becomes entangled in his sash until he can no longer move.

Heart showing mercy to even the most wretched soul. Only their own pitiful actions cause their end.

"This is the path of the dragon," says Tayo.

The rusted door opens to reveal a path to Tayo. Xi Fung looks on and screams as Tayo ascends the stairs vanishing from his sight. The door closes, and Xi Fung is left crying in the rain angrily; he is still entangled in the sash.

DRAGON

As Tayo moves upward, a light is shining very brightly. At the top, Tayo sees . . . Shy Vey.

"Welcome, young dragon Tayo," says Shy Vey, the old woman.

Ty Fong says, "Greetings, young dragon Tayo."

Tayo says, "Ty Fong, the turtle man!"

Ai Shi says, "Welcome, young dragon Tayo."

Qao Chu says, "Big Brother, hi! I knew you'd bring my doll back to me."

"The sad little kid," says Tayo.

Shao Ko says, "Yes, young dragon Tayo."

"The monk of the cave!" says Tayo.

Shao Ko says, "There is someone who's waiting to talk to you, Tayo."

"Me?" asked Tayo

Tayo goes up ahead to a huge hall where dragons entangle each other. Tayo's eyes open wide, and his mouth drops.

Moon Sing says, "Hello, Tayo."

"*Mom*," Tayo says, shocked.

Moon Sing says, "I am the shaolin dragon, my son. I hold the title, and now it's time to pass it to you."

Tayo says, "The title of shaolin dragon."

Moon Sing says, "Yes, my little Tayo. You fought Xi Fung without resorting to violence; you used your heart, mind, body, and soul. These have all led you to the path of the dragon."

Tayo says, "I understand, Mother. In each of the trials, I learned a valuable life lesson."

Ty Fong says, "Xi Fung desired power; that is all he saw. He was blinded by that one hunger. He let it consume him."

"To enter here to claim the title of shaolin dragon," says Shy Vey.

Qao Chu adds, "But you stopped him, bro."

"Now, he will remember this forever. He will never again walk the path of the dragon," says Shao Ko.

"I see," Tayo says and looks at his hands.

Moon Sing says, "Tayo, these are the sages, life teachers of lessons always to be learned of mind, body, soul, and heart."

And so, Tayo returns to his village . . ."

When he enters the village, he is dressed in his new attire, the dress of a shaolin dragon.

Shiruumi says excitedly, "You did it!"

"You beat the earth test," adds Tung Mai.

All the other kids congratulate him.

Tayo says, "*Mind, body, soul, heart*—these are the principles of everyday life, the most important lessons to be learned."

The children form a ring around the giant harvest flame. They sing, dance, and laugh. The elderly speak of when they were young and tell stories of past festivals.

Shiruumi asks, "Has anyone seen Tayo? Where has he gotten to? Tayo, where are you?"

"Hey, Shiruumi, looking for your boyfriend," Hau Rai taunts, laughing.

Shiruumi blushes and stomps off angrily, while the other children laugh. They continue to eat and drink meadow juice, a harvest festival delicacy.

Moon Sing says, "Hau Mung, I'm worried about Tayo."

Hau Mung answers, "He's with Seychinrai at the forest temple."

The moon shines brightly, illuminating two figures walking . . .

Seychinrai says, "Ah, young dragon. How do you feel, proud wielder of the shaolin?"

Tayo says, "I feel the same. Like the old me, elder."

Seychinrai responds, "Tayo, go. Go enjoy the festival; you'll understand soon, young shaolin dragon."

Tayo says, "Yes, elder."

Tayo runs to the festival, and as he does, something shocks his heart and mind.

"Pain! So much pain! It hurts so much. Mom, Dad, help!"

Tayo passes out.

Moon Sing says, "My dragon power is fading. I can't help him. He ate this fruit. Where did he get this? This is dark heart fruit. Did Xi Fung eat this as well?"

Seychinrai says, "For one so young to feel something that terrifying and horrible. He is the shaolin dragon now and must learn."

"I understand," says Moon Sing softly, "but he is my child, my baby, and I, as his mother, will protect him. Tayo, come to me. The path of the dragon will lead you back to me."

A great light erupts from them both.

"Mom," says Tayo tiredly.

Hau Mung says, "My son! Moon Sing! wake up."

Moon Sing is breathing hard and sweating. "Yes, I'm okay; I just need to rest, my husband."

Tayo remains silent.

All of a sudden, Tayo hears a voice.

"Shy Vey, is that you?" he asks.

"Young dragon," says Shy Vey, "you must return to us."

"Huh?" replied Tayo

Shao Ko says, "Your role as the shaolin dragon is more important than you think or could ever imagine."

"But my mom . . ." Tayo begins.

Shao Ko says, "She'll be fine, Tayo."

"Go! Tayo," Hau Mung says.

Tayo goes to the river, and the old sage Ty Fong is waiting for him.

"Come, Shaolin Dragon, there is much to be done," he says. Ty Fong says.

The turtle takes off in a burst of speed. As Tayo sails down the river, he senses stronger vibrations from the air and his heart.

Ty Fong says, "You feel it? It hurts, doesn't it, young dragon? You will learn what it is soon enough, young dragon Tayo."

Tayo enters the dragon temple and sees all the sages waiting for him.

Shao Ko says, "You, Tayo, are the new shaolin dragon."

"That is a heavy burden to have at such a young age," says Shy Vey.

Qao Chu says, "Yeah, bro, something's happening."

Ai Shi says, "Welcome back, kid. It's time to teach you the *true power of the dragon.*"

"True power of the dragon?" asks Tayo. "There is more. I thought this was a coming-of-age trial."

Ty Fong says, "Nope, young dragon, this is very real; it's only the tip of the iceberg."

"Are you ready, bro? This'll be the hardest thing you'll have to do in your life. Are you up to it?" asks Qao Chu.

Ai Shi says, "You felt it, didn't you, Tayo? If you don't want that to happen again, we can teach you how to combat it. Heart, mind, body, soul, and balance are only the beginning."

Shy Vey says, "You must learn how to master the seven legendary skills in order to open the path to the ultimate power that all who walk your road seek—the full might of the dragon. It is power beyond anything ever imagined. This is the power your mother used to save you."

"Mom," says Tayo with determination in his eyes.

Ty Fong says, "Let's see how long that determination lasts, young shaolin dragon."

"Don't worry about me; I'll learn this and face whatever that was," vows Tayo.

Shy Vey says, "Now that you have decided on your path, young shaolin dragon, it is time for you to venture forth and leave this place."

"Leave?" he asks.

"Yes, Shaolin Dragon," Ai Shi says, "your answers cannot be found here. The seven answers you seek lie far beyond these shores. Hurry IT is coming we must protect Tayo"

Shao Ko adds, "There is no time for good-byes, young dragon; you must leave immediately. The alarm at the village"

And so the young dragon's quest has truly begun. What new and wonderful adventures lie in store for him?

The End
or
is
it?

As Tayo rides away, the village is soon engulfed in flames of pure hate and malice. One who wears the symbol of infinity and walks with ruby silver eyes has come. The sages meet this threat and do not back down.

Seychinrai says, "So you have come. The dragon is here waiting, but to end the dragon you must first battle us"

A grand showdown explodes as the sages and the old shaolin dragon defend their land and home . . . .

THE HERO

"Wow, would you look at that! Isn't it amazing, Son, how they get these ships into the bottles?"

"Yeah, Dad," said Peter.

But Peter was not paying attention to what his father was saying. Peters eyes were focused elsewhere; he was watching the TV hero Captain Terrific perform his heroic deeds.

Captain Terrific said, "Remember, kids, be good and terrific!"

Peter said, "When I grow up, I'm going to be just like Captain Terrific, Dad."

Lucy said, "Okay, young man, time for bed."

In the morning, Peter's father Sam had a surprise: two tickets to the Captain Terrific stunt show. Peter was so excited, and as soon as Sam finished his breakfast, they were gone out the door. Peter was pushing his father. They arrived and took their seats. The show soon started, and Captain Terrific appeared in a puff of smoke.

Captain Terrific said, "Is everyone ready for a terrific show?"

The children in the crowd yelled at the top of their lungs. Captain Terrific began to wrestle the monster to the ground, but the tame bear went wild. The people panicked and ran. Peter and Captain Terrific were trapped; he tried to calm the bear down, but it was no use. Captain Terrific ran away, leaving Peter behind. Peter was crying and scared as Sam fought his way through the crowds of people. He leaped onto the stage and rushed the bear, managing to wrestle it to the ground and calm it. Peter was cradled in his father's arms.

Peter asked, "Dad, are you okay?"

Sam replied, "It's all right, Pete, just a little cut and some bruises."

But it was a hole from where the bear had bitten him in the arm. He received medical attention. The next day, the newspaper headlines read "Sam Jenkins, the Real Mr. Terrific."

Peter said, "Dad, thank you; I want to be like you when I grow up."

Sam looked at his wife and picked up his apple juice.

He said, "Thanks, Son."

The moral of this story is a hero is not all they are cracked up to be.

An investigation revealed a strange **black essence caught on the camera near the cage and was written off as static interference.**

THE GOLD

As our story starts out, we see two guys hanging around the seashore. Their names are James and Huck.

Huck said, "Looka here, James, wha' I done foun'." He slapped his knee, laughing. "I foun' me a something in this here old botta."

James replied, "Well, youse gonna open it or do I's got to drink it by my lonesome?" He licked his lips.

Huck and James opened the bottle, they saw an old worn map. James pulled it out of the bottle and unrolled it. The map looked old, but it was still readable.

"Well, woooooo-hoooooo! Look!" said James. "Huck, you know wha' this is, man?"

They looked at the map very closely. It revealed to them the fortune of a lifetime, so they quickly gathered their few belongings and Soon were off into the unknown wilderness of the desert.

The prospector said, "Well, haven't had a customer in ages. What can I do for you, gents?"

"We's ain't got much, but you can have this antique watch," said Huck.

"Hey, tha's ma watch, Huck," said James.

"Tha' thing be worthless, James. What we found is worth much more. I's gonna buy you a whole mess of watches wen we's get rich, ya hear? Now le's go."

They traded for their supplies, and were off into the humid and dry climate of the desert. They traveled deeper and deeper into the sweltering desert for days; it seemed just as they were about to run out of water, they finally reached their claim. James plopped down tired and sweating heavily.

"Wha' you doin'? Get up. There be work ta be done, hear? So you get to digging."

James said, "Hold on, Buster. Hold it right there, ya hear. I ain't digging nothin. Me feet be blistering, and I be hungry as a wolf in a sheep pasture. I's gon' eat me up some mess that there ol grub we done got get."

"We's taint got no grub," said Huck. "I finish it up way back when. You knows how I get, James, when my tummy get ta grumblin' and all."

James got mad and threw the shovel at Huck. He ducked, as the shovel hit a rock, making a strange sound. James stormed off angrily.

Huck heard the sound and discovered a small nugget of gold. He hid it, keeping it for himself. When James got back, Huck told him he didn't find anything. They dug and dug all night long. Finally, they saw all that glittered was gold in their eyes.

Huck said, "Looka there, James. All the gold we's could ever need in all our lives, hooooo boy!" he said, slapping his knee. "This is it, buddy. We's on easy street now." He laughed.

James whistled.

But the gold was on a fault line and an earthquake was coming.

Huck said, "Take as much as you can carry."

"James, this is our ticket to fortune and the good old life, hooooooooo!"

"Look," said James, "I'm doing the bes' I can now, so hush up and skedaddle. Go on get ya Hear me? Get. Scoot scoot."

They grabbed sack loads of gold and departed, but they were moving too slow. Soon, the earthquake hit.

Huck said, "Run, James. Come on; shake a leg!"

"Huck," said James, "I can't go on. This here gold's too heavy on ma bones."

He dropped the sacks of gold and ran as the earth trembled beneath them. Huck left him behind as the ground began to split open. James was hanging on for dear life.

"Huck!" he yelled. "Help, please! I can't get up! Help! You there?"

Huck was thinking hard. He dropped his sacks of gold and extended his hand to save James. His gold sacks began to slip away from him; he was watching the sacks slide away little by little at the same time he had his hand extended. His eyes kept shifting between the gold and James. The hole was getting bigger as the sand was pouring in much faster now. Huck looked at James and then at the sacks of gold. He did this three times. Finally, he pulled his friend up. They managed to escape with their lives.

James said, "We done made it out alive Huck. I reckon we be a couple lucky muskrats, huh, you sly old fox? You had me there. I thought you gonna choose that old gold over yer friend."

"It be that gold fever that be a gotten in ma blood; that wicked ol' greed monster had a spell over me in its grip. I had ta break loose and see ma friend. Sorry, James, for being a doggone fool. Friends forever?" Huck said while rubbing his eyes

"Friends forever," said James. "You know what, Huck? It's time we's find real jobs and get edumacated."

"Hoooooo!" said Huck. "Doggone, if you ain't right!" He laughed.

The moral of this story is greed is a monster that consumes all if it is allowed; true friendship is golden and rarer than any kind of money.

THE FOX

Have you ever heard the old sayings "sly as a fox" and "you can't outfox a fox"? Well, that's true—or sort of, that is.

By the way, our heroine's name is Shirley. She was on her way home when she saw a fox. It was lying under a tree. It had a whole bunch of candy in bags.

Fox said, "Oh this. This is my treasure I've gathered up for all these years. But what I'm looking for is the legendary cherry cherry candies."

Now, Shirley had some candy too. She looked at her hand and saw she had a bag of cherry cherry candies.

Fox said, "I would give all this candy away just to have a taste of those." Fox looked at her out of the corner of his eye.

Shirley looked at her bag and compared it to Fox's great treasure bags.

Shirley said, "Hey, Mister Fox, I'll trade you this bag of cherry cherry candies for that treasure of yours. How bout it?"

"Really?" Fox shouted with excitement. "Fine, then it's a deal. You can have all of my candy, and I get yours. Okay, girlie."

Now, Shirley never noticed the fox's tails. It had five of them. So the fox took the cherry cherry candies.

Fox said, "Thanks, kid. Uhhhhh, my foot hurts. I'll be off now, okay."

The fox vanished into the sunset, when all of a sudden a storm came along, and Shirley wasn't able to move all of her newfound candy treasure.

Storm Storm said, "Ha, ha, ha, I see candies to be blown away!"

Whoosh, whoosh, the wind blew with its mighty breath, and down came a storm of rain. As the rain fell, the candy's color began to wash off, only to reveal Ping-Pong balls.

Shirley cried. "He tricked me! That fox tricked me." She cried even harder.

She was soaking wet as the rain fell, and the storm continued. The Ping-Pong balls blew away. Just then, a wagon appeared carrying a man in a black top hat with silver trim around it. The wagon stopped, and the man dismounted. He saw the little girl. He introduced himself to her.

Top Hat said, "Greetings, salutations, and permissions of all sorts, my dear little lady," with a smile to rival the sun.

As Top Hat was saying all of this, his top hat opened to give her flowers. His gloves made small suns and rainbows appear, making happy faces. She stopped crying and started laughing. Top Hat inspected the area.

Top Hat said, "I see a fox has troubled you with his tricky trickery of tricks, and the trick this time is candies that are so yum yummy yummery. How many tails did he have, my dear child?"

"Let me see now," said Shirley. "One, two, three, four, *five*."

As she counted, Top Hat turned his body into the numbers she said to help her.

Shirley said, "Five, the fox had five tails."

Top Hat said, "I see a five-tailed fox stole or rather tricked you out of your candy. Well now, let's see what we can do about finding a five-tailed fox and getting your candy back. Climb aboard, matey; we shove off now. Chum chummery." The horse grew wings and took off as the wagon transformed into a suitcase. Her eyes were amazed.

Top Hat said, "Well, here we go. You use my patented thinga-ma-bobber doohickey detector. HA ha with this, we'll find that fox."

They found the fox, but he was tied to a tree.

Shirley said, "Mean old fox."

Top Hat said, "So, Five Tails, looks like the fox has been outfoxed."

Fox said, "Please, let me go; I won't trick or steal anymore."

Top Hat said, "So I see you got into trouble, Fox. Hmmmmmm, looks like someone's going to eat you." He waved his finger in a way, telling the fox, "Shame on you."

"Who wants to eat him?" asked Shirley.

Top Hat said, "Well now, we have a grumph. They eat five-tailed foxes."

"A grumph?" asked Shirley.

Top Hat answered, "Yup, a grumph."

A huge grumph appeared. It was a massive creature, the size of a building.

Grumph said, "He who stops a grumph gets a wopping ol' garumph thump."

Top Hat said, "Well now, Mr. Grumph. This fox here is no good; surely if you eat him, he'll give you a big bad tummy twirler."

Grumph said, "No good fox is you say, Hat Man? Then I eat you and little girl."

Top Hat put his hands on his chin, thinking. "How 'bout this? Look at you; you're not a lean, mean grumph machine, Mister Grumph. Too much fatty food and not enough exercise. See, Shirley, that's why it's good to exercise and eat right. Stay away from candy. Right, Teeth?"

Teeth said, "Yeah, Top Hat."

A little tooth man appeared from behind Top Hat's leg.

Teeth said, "Whoa, Mister Grumph, look at those cavities!"

Grumph said, "Grumph teeth do hurt a lot lately—pain bad, very bad."

"Well now, Grumph," said Top Hat, "I can fix that. Right, Teeth?"

Teeth said, "Sure thing, Top Hat."

"Shirley, my suitcase, please, if you will," said Top Hat.

She handed him the suitcase, and it began to transform into Doctor Teeth's Miracle Spectacular Fantastic Super-Duper Sprinkles-on-Top Dentist Office and Spa.

Teeth said, "Step into my office, big guy. We'll fix you right up."

The grumph stepped in, and many hours later . . .

Grumph emerged and said, "Grumph feel great, like new grumph."

"Well, I try," Teeth said and laughed.

Top Hat said, "Well now, see what I told you, big guy."

A big screen popped out of Top Hat's hat.

Teeth said, "Okay, here we go. Now remember to brush and floss. Stay away from fatty foods. Drink plenty of liquids, and be healthy."

Top Hat's dental office turned into a rocket ship, blasting off.

Top Hat said, "Well, Mister Fox, I hope you learned a lesson."

The rocket ship landed, and everyone exited the ship.

Fox said, "Sorry, Shirley."

Top Hat said, "So, everybody, let's have some."

...fox . . . I hear you calling to me, ... and be with you. It has been a long time since we had ...on."

Top Hat revealed her face; she wasn't a man fox at all but a female fox that had gray whiskers. The hat covered her, slowly vanishing.

The End

M's Log 95XX
About the Author

Michael R. Welch has been writing stories since he was in the third grade. He remembered the old stories that he had written long ago, which inspired him to finish this book. Many characters have spun off into their own stories to stand alone during their adventures.

Michael was born in the Bronx, New York, area in a rough neighborhood. Having an imagination helped him to see that it could be a great place to discover hidden wonders right in front of his eyes. Yet even to this day, there are still more wonders that need to be found. Michael hopes the spirit of the adventurer continues to develop, leading future wanderers to *touch the sky one day*!

Living in the Bronx was never boring; something was always happening that gave him the inspiration to dream of a better tomorrow.

I've been sailing the sea of stars with my crew aboard me ship for countless years. Aye, we've had our fair share of ups and downs through the cosmos, but I will say to thee having mates ye can count on in any dire back-to-the-wall battle beats riches and bounty any day.

So, are ye ready to leave home port for the mysteries of creation?

"Life is the greatest adventure. Are ye ready to raise anchor and set sail?"

Michael R. Welch

The Final Chronicle Log

Till we dream again . . .

Did you believe the truth of what was written earlier?
An evil one is capable of many things, but thank goodness, we of
the light exist to unravel his or her dark deeds. Now, dear reader, I
show you the *truth*.

Recap

Grail Ra screamed, "The light! The light! No, I hate the light! Get
away from me!" He burned up. "Nooooo!" he yelled in pain.

Grail Ra fell smoking and hurt. He did not move.

"All five are here at last. I am the bearer of light. I am Samantha
Alrous Crystala, princess of Deserna. My friend Clockwork Knight
left his legacy to me. I take up the Grail Imperium lance blade."

The Old Caretaker said, "Ma'am, your prize awaits thee."

"The light told me of Igneous's dark ambitions and of Grail Ra's
treachery. Now I take the lead. *Torloc xhioc roc no tore!*" she said.

In an instant, the gems appeared, as each one began to drain away from them. The Loom Rubies appeared before Samantha. The Old Caretaker escorted her to the king's hall. They walked the halls and finally approached the barrier that surrounded the Pagama lord's throne.

The Caretaker said, "Go on, young girl; approach what is now your destiny. Claim your radiance, and usher us into an age of platinum."

Samantha Alrous Crystala approached the king's throne with the four jewels shining an illuminating light, as four beams shot out, penetrating the barrier. Then, the fifth jewel of lights beam shot out. The king's barrier was gone.

The Caretaker said, "Now the throne will judge you, deeming you worthy."

A light engulfed her, drawing her closer. The Loom Rubies began to come together as one. A symbol of Loom began to appear around her. It was a majestic light. All of a sudden, a blast of dark energy hit her, making her fall to the ground unconscious.

Diabolical laughter rang out.

"At last! Now I shall ascend the Pagama lord's throne and rule on high as a god!" The evil laughter stopped abruptly. "*What*? How did you escape my blast, girl?"

Samantha said, "Not so, black spirit; the light has warned me of your tricks, and now out of arrogance, you reveal your true face, Fortune-Teller."

Fortune-Teller said, "So you would challenge me—one who is as old as time itself and surely more skilled than a mere child who is but a novice? Ack!"

Samantha hit him with a light arrow attack as he was speaking.

Then Corsx and Hagglesbee ran into the throne room area only to see the Caretaker, Samantha, and the mysterious person.

An evil laugh echoed loudly

Corsx asked, "Caretaker?"

Hagglesbee called out, "Samantha, is that you? I thought you were dead, killed by the assassins!"

"*Brother*!" Samantha shouted.

A giant black beast arose from the husk of the Fortune-Teller Samantha had hit before. It looked at them like they were tiny insects.

"*Roar*! You will die in excruciating pain!" Fortune-Teller laughed.

G asked, "Is this a private party, or can anyone join? Yee-haw. I guess this thing in front of us is the real bad guy, huh?"

Fortune-Teller said, "Another insect to feast upon and soul to energize me!"

The beast mouth opened with deadly acidic saliva dripping from its fangs.

Till we dream again . . .

G said, "Okay, Fire Ruby, let's rock—and none of your crud, all right? I'm back in control of my body at last. That other presence was suffocating me, like it was trying to erase who I was and devour my soul. Ruby, I need your power. Rahhhhhh!"

G punched the air, sending huge flame spirals shooting out and damaging the Fortune-Teller beast. He had the beast on the ropes and pinned down, Corsx set up a geyser blast from underneath, but the Fortune-Teller beast took flight, transforming into a giant shadow-beast dragon. The Fortune-Teller dragon sprayed the area with poisonous muck. The horrid substance began to emit a toxic vapor that ate away at the floor; however, a mysterious individual used the Earth Ruby power to hold the ground together with gigantic rock hands, and then he launched a huge rock fist into the air. The individual signaled to the ruby bearers to jump.

Hagglesbee used his wind spirals to create an air disk so they could land safely. The fortune beast saw them firing poisonous purple flames that attempted to consume them, but Hagglesbee created a vortex funnel that reflected its blast back toward the Fortune-Teller beast.

Not realizing their plan, the beast went in for the kill. Corsx and Samantha were concealed in the air bubble covered by the purple flames, and as the beast stood to launch its own attack, Corsx and Samantha emerged to counter. Samantha used light whips to ensnare the Fortune-Teller beast hanging on to it so that Corsx would not be poisoned when he touched it.

The Fortune-Teller beast roared in agony as the light burned at its wicked and decomposing flesh; soon, the ones consumed by their wicked deeds could be seen trying to grab and drag them in. Samantha intensified the light, combining it with her heart.

Corsx stood firm, ready to use his water abilities. He formed water blades to peel the beast's skin open, but the beast began to spin in a tornado to shake them off. The Fortune-Teller beast did something that surprised them; it soon transformed again.

Hagglesbee called out, "Samantha, Corsx, G!"

G said, "Now what? Whoa, man, some days, it just doesn't pay to be a treasure hunter."

A black shadow serpent arose. Its ruby eyes looked at G, giving him a piercing, instant-death vibe.

G yelled, "Come and get it, scale bag!"

G's eyes began to turn a bright orange, his hair became flames, and his muscles increased in size.

"*Igneous cannon*!" yelled G.

The Igneous cannon is a powered flame beam in the form of pure anger, hate, and apathy.

Soon, the snake beast was engulfed in horrid flames. It screamed in agony.

G laughed insanely. "None shall stand against my power. You think you are darkness? Please! Don't waste my time, garbage."

Samantha said, "G . . . wake up!"

"Foolish child," said G, his voice echoing. "Prepare for an unpleasant end and be honored to be granted a merciful, quick death from your god!"

Samantha silently prayed, *Oh, soothing calm, aid my hand. Guide my heart; return those fallen to madness's reach.*

"What?" shouted G. "Let me go! I command you!"

Corsx and the earth bearer held G with ice and earth arms. G fell as the powered Igneous soul was finally released from the ruby of flame.

Igneous laughed. "Hahahaha! Free at last! Now it's time to really turn up the heat! Die!"

"Oh crap!" said Corsx. "I hope this was part of yer plan, kid."

"You!" said Hagglesbee. "I remember you. You were there when—"

"When our father was murdered!" finished Samantha.

"Silly, foolish mortals trying to hold a god," said Igneous. "Your family bound me and then tried to use my power to rule. However, I decided to teach them a lesson. Are you sure your father is dead, boy? If I recall, your blood boils just like mine. Can you feel it? The sensation of pure battle, fighting . . . and you, girl, what of you?"

Samantha said, "Are you saying that we're your children, that we're half gods? You're no god!"

Hagglesbee added, "You are only a murderer. Coward!"

"Tsk, tsk. Deserna, hmm? *What*? No!" said Igneous.

Igneous fell to his knees, weakened.

Michael R Welch

He said, "You? Who are you? How are you able to invoke the seal of creation?" Igneous yelled while in pain.

"Never mind that, Emperor of Flame. Just know you are beaten this day." said the mysterious individual.

Corsx said, "Nice job."

Hagglesbee added, "You have my thanks."

Samantha asked, "My ruby . . . you are an enemy?"

"What?" asked Hagglesbee.

Corsx said, "Earth bearer."

"We're not done yet," said mysterious individual. "Don't let your guard down, and be alert; ruby bearers, can you feel it?"

Fortune-Teller gasped. "My shadow arts, eh? Hahahahaha! My gratitude for sealing that pest! Now I can end your lives myself and claim the stones for my own."

He changed into a huge beast octopus with sixty-eight eyes and eight hundred sixty six tentacles. The eyes shot out black beams while the tentacles bombarded the area as the castle crumbled around them.

Corsx said, "Gotta be away to take him down. He is like a shadow, but we bearers can hurt him somehow."

Hagglesbee suddenly shouted, "I got it!"

An earth shield arose.

The shield was blocking the bombarding arms from causing any more damage by growing thick stone on them and increasing their weight. Corsx then encased the rock in ice and shot off millions of ice spikes that impaled the Fortune-Teller octotruga hagis beast.

Lady who illuminates the charge, Samantha prayed, *rain down your divine touch.*

A light beam burst through the darkened sky, piercing the black, haunting miasma, and pummeled the beast, revealing the Fortune-Teller once more.

Corsx asked, "You had enough?"

Fortune-Teller spoke in a raspy, deep, decaying voice. "So these are the bearers. Suitable souls to sacrifice, they have proven. It appears the Loom rubies are or have bonded with them."

Hagglesbee said, "He can hardly hold his state. He is breaking apart. We've won."

Fortune-Teller said, "Really, fool, we of the dark arts are formidable. Your parlor tricks are nothing. Prepare to go to oblivion, to our master."

"What's going on?" Corsx asked. "The castle is shaking."

Hagglesbee said, "He's opened a portal!"

Samantha, holding the light ruby, said, "He is planning to sacrifice your souls and the gems."

"Time has run out; we have to get to the Tower of Terra to stabilize the planet, or we're all dead. Let him have the palace. Hagglesbee, quick!" said the mysterious person.

Hagglesbee set up tornadoes so everyone could ride out safely. But the Fortune-Teller would not stop.

Corsx said, "We're still novices in using our powers; if we want to stand a chance, we have to go full power up and become the rubies themselves."

Hagglesbee said, "We can't do that; we'll die. I became the wind, and it felt like something was pulling me from the mortal plain."

"Then I suggest you end this test of your bearer powers or else your ventures will have been in vain to you and your comrades." Said the mysterious person.

Samantha asked, "What do I do?"

Light Ruby asked, "Do you believe? Pagama."

Samantha said, "Pagama?"

Corsx said, "Pagama is courage. It means courage."

"Who of you will bear the might of a god or goddess? Speak!" the mysterious person said boldly

The portal opened wider, consuming the land and part of the sea around it. The horrid souls could be seen and heard, arising from the depths of eternal darnation.

Hagglesbee said, "I just found you after all this time, and you're the only family I have left. I . . . I . . . I . . . can't lose you all over again, Apples."

"Can you sacrifice him, child? Can you alone wield the power of the gods—no, this universe's might? Can you *ascend*?" the mysterious man asked.

Samantha said sorrowfully, "Hagglesbee . . ."

Fortune-Teller laughed insanely. "Your precious Deserna was consumed, hahahahaaha! All those souls wicked and innocent are now fueling me. Your people were quite stupid and easy to fool. It was a pleasure to devour them. The beast of the night enjoyed defiling and devouring each piece of their souls down to the last delicious inch, OH HOW THEY SCREAMED IN AGONY, TERROR, PAIN. THEIR EXCRUCIATING MOMENTS WERE PURE EUPHORIA"

As they flew toward the Tower of Terra, the Fortune-Teller gargonus pursued them.

The Fortune-Teller gargonus was a grotesque creature that ate any living thing's energy and then converted it to negative and malicious energy. The souls of the planet were being absorbed along with any Mappers caught in the cross fire as smaller battles began erupting across the planet for survival.

Corsx said, "I'll buy you some time, kiddo."

"Stand steadfast and ever vigilant; follow the banner that waves forever *true*." the mysterious person replied.

Samantha said, "Wait! I know it can't be; you're . . ."

"To battle, Corsx, we go." said the mysterious person bravely.

They unleashed their ruby powers full force and attacked the dead, resentful beasts that had hate and malice in their core. The beasts of the apocalypse fell groaning as they kept coming with their hunger even more feverish.

Meanwhile, Hagglesbee and Samantha were under attack.

Samantha yelled, "Hagglesbee!"

"Samantha, no!" he shouted. "Back off, you scum; don't you touch her!"

He let loose a barrage of wind attacks, cutting them all down. He fell to his knees, exhausted, as Samantha ran to his side and created a light barrier. The onslaught continued as more beasts appeared to devour them while the Fortune-Teller gargonus looked on with delight.

As all hope seemed lost, a blast came from out of nowhere, hitting the dead beasts and the Fortune-Teller gargonus.

Relse said, "Aye, I see you're in need of help, right, Captain? The others are here as well."

Corsx said, "Tch . . . Who knew?"

The dead were being beaten around the field by a young lad with a dragon emblem.

Tayo said, "You must live. This creature, it possessed Xi Fung, a person I once called a friend, and fed on his rage . . . I can hear and see it now, Samantha of the Olmgala."

Pete said, "Yes, this creature tried to kill me in the past to prevent me from meeting you here and now."

Samantha asked, "But who?"

Pete said, "We meet years later."

Tayo added, "Yes, today is a special day."

They continued to fight and talk.

Huck said, "Yep, we's pleased to meet you."

Corsx relplied," you got to be kidding me, wow here and now another mapper mystery I wanted to solve is finished".

James added, "We ain't supposed to meet till you grown like ol' tree."

Fox agreed, "Quite. We heard your cry through time, and here we are on this special *day*."

"It is sure good to see you all." Said the mysterious person.

Everyone said, "Aye, aye."

"You've been well missed." Said the mysterious person.

Samantha asked, "I?"

Hagglesbee said, "I understand today is."

G said, "Deathclaim."

The Fortune-Teller gargonus said, "I will sacrifice you all to his majesty and be granted more power. Oh what a delicious hunger. Power. Die! Die! Die!"

"Go, and, here, take this. I don't need it any longer." He threw the earth ruby to Corsx. "Get to the tower ASAP. Oh and get the kid up here for a minute." said the mysterious person.

Zornogoya said, "Gracious one who showers us, bestow your faith in our alms."

As she cast this over the area, light rods burst from the ground impaling the wicked ones.

Wanshreemu said, "By the nightfall's moon, I invoke thy yell, King of the Midnight Moon."

Ghost beast wolves emerged to aid the caster in their hour of need.

The field was being cleansed but the gargonus still remained.

The ship headed for the tower while the crew took on the massive horde.

They reached the tower and were permitted to enter. Samantha, Corsx, and Hagglesbee looked around at the massive structure.

Hagglesbee said, "We're out of time, and evil is at the door. So where do we go from here? Samantha?"

She walked in the direction of an old well and pressed a stone revealing the way to the ruby chamber.

Hagglesbee said, "It's a trance of some kind."

Corsx said, "According to the mural, like I saw in the Ice Citadel, we have to become the stabilizers since we have the rubies."

G said, "That's crap, man! We'll die; what's the point?"

Hagglesbee asked, "Where's my sister? No!"

Corsx said, "We already used our ruby power and exhausted ourselves there's no turning back now. We have to hurry before we fade away.

Samantha had already stepped into the ruby accelerator and vanished. They did the same and saw the *truth*.

Meanwhile, outside . . .

The gargonus yelled, "*No, no, no!*"

Samantha appeared with the Olmgala Crystal as her heart and was a *true goddess*. She looked at the Fortune-Teller gargonus, and it crumbled to star dust. She closed her eyes. A tear fell, cleansing the planet and returning the horrid rancid souls from whence they came—or rather they had now been put to rest after eons of torment. Their soul flares littered the atmosphere of the planet Pagama.

"Your Majesty Apples Alrous Crystala, or I should say *Lady Olmgala.*"

Lady Olmgala spoke from her mind. She knew to whom the ship and crew belonged.

"I understand *everything now*. Few are lucky enough to see or grasp this, and then there are those who dream of having this. You once had this and gave it back, splitting it once more. This planet, I can see its history and why the elders praise the *savior* so much. He came to Deserna once long ago and helped not just our father but our people and our universe. The one true lord of the Pagama people, I see him too. So much to see, where do I start? You saw this, and you have even sailed there. You truly are *him*, aren't you?"

"Yes. Yes, I am. Few people can actually find me. They say I'm a story and a myth or legend, but I stand before you real. You are a goddess now. What will you do with this gift?"

Lady Olmgala said, "Your ship is the P—"

"Yes." replied the mysterious man.

"You could have beaten that monster, Fortune-Teller, easily; I foresaw it. You truly are that strong. This power granted you strength. But you gave that back and chose to use your original might. How could you be on that level? Even as a goddess, I cannot comprehend. Is it because I am a godling? I am still very much a newborn. There's so much suffering, and you have beaten evil countless times to bring peace. I can hear so many and see them from here. My brother and family are gone. They are not in the realm of the dead; they are gone from creation forever."

Zornogoya said, "You may use the claim to wish them back or go to the sacred place in creation where many venture but few make it. The GATE. If you are in so much pain, then use your power to bring them back and others—become a savior."

"You have all eternity to decide what you want to do, Lady Olmgala. Deathclaim is the day that one can see one's deceased loved ones; however, foolish people and beasts used it to gain power. It has been a long time since it was used for good."

Lady Olmgala said, "Having this power is not a toy; it is a responsibility."

"I see." said the mysterious man.

Zornogoya said, "Really? You think so. You can do anything you *want*."

Wanshreemu said, "You're fifteen years old with the power of a goddess. You can be older or stay young and beautiful forever. You could have the universe if you so wished or make your own."

Samantha said, "No, that's all selfish. If I have this power and others have loved ones who pass on but can never have such a power, then . . ."

"Then?" said the mysterious man.

Samantha said, "I choose . . ."

Riiiiiiiiiiiiiiiiiiiiiiiiiiiiiiiinnnnnnnnnnnnnnnnng!

"Hey, sleepy head, wake up. Class is over, and you managed to sleep through yet another class. Hmmm, how do you expect to get through school with grades like these?"

Samantha said, "Oh man! I had this dream I was adventuring through the stars. I was the lost princess of a kingdom, and I became a goddess. Wow, I'm hungry." Her stomach rumbled.

Tisha said, "Uh, yeah. Whatever!" She laughed hysterically.

Mr. Hagglesbee said, "If you're going to sleep in class, at least try not to snore, Miss Waters."

Samantha said, "Sorry, Mister—I mean Brother. So what is for dinner?"

Hagglesbee said, "Don't know. What do you feel like eating apple (her nick name)?"

After eating dinner, they went for their evening jog and saw the people Samantha had met in her dream working at different jobs.

They made it home, and Samantha finished her homework. She stared at her crystal pendant before she fell asleep.

A shooting star could be seen near Samantha's position from space.

But from afar, a person wearing a black suit and hat with a cane looked up and spoke.

Mr. Leginshire laughed as he walked away. "I'll get you another day, girl. Another day."

There is always a warning; if you ever meet the Leginshire man, beware before it is time for him to ***collect***.

This is the end of one journey but the beginning of another . . .

About the Book

Mystical phantasia is set in the year 5795. This is but one
of the many flash back tales that have been recorded in the mappers
journal logs from adventuerers who have sat around camp fires
sharing their memories and food with others in the vast frontier of
space. Earth enjoys a platinum age of great utopian peace along
with the rest of the northern universe where it is located.

Now brave adventurers and treasure seekers hope to find Platinum
M the king of thieves treasure which is said among old sea dogs to
be worth trillions.They also seek his legendary ship so they can sail
to the threshold of creation having their most cherished wish
granted.

MYSTICAL PHANTASIA
19TH ANNIVERSARY

WE THANK ALL OF THE FANS FOR
FOLLOWING US FROM THE BEGINNING.